AF663321

Golden Tree

And Other Stories

notionpress.com

Golden Tree

And Other Stories

Rayasam Muralidhar

notionpress.com

Notion Press

Old No. 38, New No. 6

McNichols Road, Chetpet

Chennai - 600 031

First Published by Notion Press 2015

ISBN 978-93-5206-602-5

Dedicated to Women

particularly those in Sonagachi and other

red light areas of the world

CONTENTS

FOREWORD

Putting Pen to Paper is something I have always done, though for my own pleasure. Words fascinate me for the sheer power they have in conveying different things to different people at different times. They not only have the power to touch lives but change them too. They evoke a variety of emotions – joy, sorrow, pain, fear, hatred, compassion and love to name just a few.

The habit of reading from a young age must have kindled my fascination for words, whether they are written, said or sung.

Another reason for my habit of reading and writing could be the fact that it runs in the family.

I have always shared the joy of reading and writing with my wife who shares my passion for words.

As usual, when I read my story 'Golden Tree', she liked it and insisted that I publish it. That is how I decided to put the Paper to Public view and that is how my first book has landed in your hands.

Happy Reading

GOLDEN TREE

Chapter 1

STRANGE NOISES

Monday; May 25, 2009

Kolkata

Premnath sat patiently waiting for a customer. Not a soul was to be seen on the street. It was not very late though. It was only 10 past 5. So he still had some hope. He wondered when the rains would stop. It was the fifth day since the torrential rains had started. In the last 4 days there had hardly been a dozen customers. He looked at the cash in the counter again. It remained the same dismal 100 odd rupees. It didn't bother him much because he had seen worse times in the fifty years of his life.

It was 37 years ago that he had run away from Meerut with fifty rupees in his pocket and traveling ticketless reached Delhi. He made the streets of Paharganj his home which felt heavenly compared to the life in the slums of Tarapuri back home. He worked as a cleaner in several road side restaurants in Tooti Gali, Nehru Bazaar, Chuna Mandi and the Main Bazaar. Then slowly he graduated to a waiter and a Tea master after learning the art of making tea and improving his skills to become a much sought after master. Life in Paharganj was not easy but it was better than the hell he had left behind which kept haunting him in his dreams.

Sometimes he dreamt of his early childhood, the only part of his slum life worth remembering. His father was a rickshaw puller who toiled hard the whole day to make enough money to feed and clothe his family. He also supported his brother whom he tried to educate but in vain. He turned out to be a ruffian and goonda, yet he was scared of his elder brother. Premnath was the apple of his eye and he loved him dearly. When Premnath turned five, he was sent to the local school. His father took keen interest in his studies and encouraged him to learn on his own as well. So he bought for his son illustrated story books. Premnath enjoyed all the attention and love his father showered on him.

Suddenly there was a heavy flash of lightning followed by a deafening thunder bringing Premnath back to the present with a jolt. It was pouring heavily now. Premnath looked at the clock, one of his first possessions which had ticked along all these years without any repairs. He had bought it in old Delhi for Rs. 25/-. It was 9 O'clock. Just when he thought of shutting shop, he saw some movement down the street. As he wondered who had ventured out on such a night, he saw the faint light of a two wheeler and a dark figure atop. The bike stopped outside his shop and a man in a dripping rain coat ran into his shop and removed his helmet. Premnath took an instant dislike to him as he thought the man was mean. He was tall, well built and even handsome in a crooked way. He stood there seemingly sizing up Premnath, his shop and the surroundings. Premnath broke the silence and enquired how he could help him.

"What a night, has it been raining like this all day?" enquired the man. "All week," replied Premnath. He didn't like the man's voice either. So he said a little testily, "I was closing shop, do you need anything?" The man saida little sarcastically,

"So early, and that too in this area." He then said, "Can I have a cup of tea?" Premnath vanished behind the curtain. The man extended his hand to pick up some biscuits from the glass jar. "Wait," said Premnath before the man could even touch the jar. He was back with a cup of steaming hot tea. He took out a couple of biscuits, placed them in a saucer and gave it to the man. "That was pretty fast," the man said.

He then asked not taking his eyes off Premnath, "Where can I find Pinto?"

"I don't know any Pinto," said Premnath.

"How long have you been here," the man enquired.

"None of your business," replied Premnath a little gruffly.

The man realized he was getting nowhere with this guy but no one else was in sight. So he took his time with his tea and biscuits. Premnath reminded him that he was closing his shop and gestured him to get going. The man paid for the tea and biscuits and reluctantly stepped out. Even before he could put his helmet on, Premnath shut the shop muttering to himself, 'what a bad lot'. But then good lots don't come to such places, thought Premnath. Though the business was dull, he could do without such customers, he thought.

The man put on his helmet, started the bike and drove slowly along the street looking for the guy he wanted. The tea was good and warmed him up but not the tea shop fellow. The man knew that the fellow knew Pinto but he wouldn't talk. He didn't like the way the fellow treated him. 'He will feel sorry one day' said the man to himself.

The rain got heavier and Premnath hoped his shack would survive the night. He sat down to his meal of rotis and potatoes (aloo dum). He wondered what the slime was upto on such a night. But the place was home to such characters. It gave them a means of livelihood. Premnath couldn't complain of the place that had sheltered and sustained him for 30 years since he left Paharganj and made this place his home. The place always kept him busy all night and filled his coffers. It was this cyclone that had ruined the business for the last 5 days. He reminded himself that he was not alone. Everyone in the area or for that matter the whole city suffered business loss. Cyclones are impartial. They don't spare any one. It will soon pass and it will be business as usual.

His thoughts drifted back to the lone visitor that night and his enquiries about Pinto. He thought the joker must be some pimp for some dirty woman. He hated all women. They reminded him of his mother.

Even though it was too early to go to bed, he made his bed on the benches that served to seat the customers during business hours and lay down. He normally retired at 4.00 a.m and woke up by 8.00. As he lay there listening to the continuous sounds of lightning, thunder, incessant rain and the heavy winds, he dozed off and drifted back to the slums of Tarapuri.

It was raining heavily and Premnath was totally drenched and exhausted. He had looked for work everywhere the whole day but in vain. He returned home hungry and defeated. As he entered the house, he was stunned to see his mother lying half naked with his uncle. She screamed at him to get out. Hastily he came out and stood there motionless in the pouring rain. Suddenly he got a severe jolt as his uncle kicked him with his foot. Premnath fell down but before he could get up, his uncle started kicking him. Luckily, he found a large stone by his side. He picked it up and threw it at his uncle. It landed on his head and he fell like a sack. Premnath didn't know whether the man was dead or had just fainted. He quickly searched his pockets and found some cash which he transferred to his own pocket. The sudden silence brought his mother out. Finding her lover lying like a log, she started screaming at Premnath. Hurling abuses she started pelting him with whatever stones she could lay her hands on. He shouted back calling her a whore and a witch and threw some stones back at her. Then he saw his uncle stir. The commotion also brought others out of their shacks. Premnath realized that if he was caught, he would be beaten to death. So he ran blindly into the rain. He somehow reached the railway station. He found a train in the yard dark and empty. He tried several doors and finally found one that opened. He just crawled under a seat and hid himself. He lay there shivering and crying and didn't know when he dozed off.

He suddenly woke up and found himself in his shop. He was sweating despite the heavy rains outside. He cursed his mother, uncle and the nightmare that continued to haunt him even after all these years. He was not sure whether they were dead or alive and didn't care. The nightmare left his throat dry and the body soaked in sweat. It always had this effect on him. He drank some water, patted himself dry with the gumtcha[1] and went back to bed.

It continued to rain heavily outside as he lay there feeling feverish and slowly drifting into a fitful sleep. He heard strange noises of beating, abuses, cries and screams. He couldn't make out whether it was all happening out on the street or inside his head. Finally it was all quiet, calm and peaceful and totally dark. He had finally fallen into a deep slumber.

---

1 Gumtcha: thin and soft hand woven cotton towel (mostly red in colour) popular in West Bengal and other eastern states of India.

Chapter 2

THE ABDUCTION

Sunday; May 24, 2009

Hyderabad

Ram Manohar Rao, IPS was a tough cop. The DCP was much feared and respected by the bosses and the ranks as well. He was honest, clean and ruthless in dealing with crime and criminals. The gangs loathed him. Their political connections didn't purchase any favours from the DCP. Since his posting as the head of the crime branch, crime rate in the city had come down and the goonda elements kept a low profile. They were seething to settle scores with him.

Rao knew this only too well. His wife Nandini was a beautiful woman and a brilliant engineer. She worked as a chief executive in one of the top notch companies and was a highly regarded professional. The company besides providing all amenities took care of her security as well. So Rao didn't have to worry about her.

Their daughter Swapnachitra, fondly called Sapna was ravishingly beautiful. She was about 10 times more beautiful than her mother was when she was of the same age. Sapna was all of 20, stood 5' 10" tall and had the figure of Venus. Surprisingly she had a sweet voice too. Sapna was aware of her looks and the effect it had on people especially the ones of the opposite gender. She became conscious of it quite early and even as a child developed the tact to be modest, simple and unassuming so that she could interact with others easily without any airs. So she got along very well with her school and college mates who adored her without envy. The fact that she was the daughter of a high profile cop also helped in keeping unwanted elements away. Yet the father knew that she would be the prime target of the underworld. But being righteous and clean, he did not want to use the official machinery to provide security to his daughter. So he hired Sanjay Kumar Saxena, an Ex-Serviceman as her chauffeur and body guard. He was not only a good driver but an excellent soldier who knew precisely what to do in case of an emergency.

Sapna had managed to keep many a handsome suitor at bay and nip in the bud their advances with a firm and polite NO. As fate would have it she fell for the most unlikely guy one day. He was tall, pale and gaunt. He believed in simple living and high thinking and practiced it too. He was the only son of a couple engaged in social work. They worked for an NGO that ran orphanages and old age homes. She first met him during the college debate in which they were pitched on opposite sides. She was bowled over by his simplicity, humility, compassion, clear thoughts, strong views and eloquence in speech. He single handedly won the debate for his team. So for the first time she made the approach – until then it was always the men who approached her.

Suresh Babu liked her instantly for her good nature and lack of airs despite her high profile family background and her exceptional beauty. Sapna being what she was didn't wait for the word to get around to her parents. She told them the same night without beating around the bush. They appreciated her sincerity and straight forward approach. They gave their consent to pursue her friendship with him for then. Rao immediately had a thorough but discreet background check done on the boy and his parents. Though they found them to be too simple for their comfort and had their doubts about how Sapna would fit into such a lifestyle, they let her continue her friendship with the boy. The two met regularly and visited a particular cafe for chatting over snacks and coffee. Their friendship had matured into love and they were now madly in love. Sapna's parents were now worried and so was Suresh. His parents discouraged him, though they had nothing against Sapna or her family. They knew the ways of the rich and powerful and so were scared of them. They didn't want their only son to get hurt emotionally and so were very worried. Rao was also equally worried about his only daughter. He sometimes felt that he should never have encouraged it in the first place. Her frequent meetings with Suresh and the long hours they spent together constantly worried him and so Rao instructed Sanjay to be more vigilant and regularly report everything to him more frequently. Rao also alerted his regular informants to keep an eye and report regularly. Sanjay did not know about this. This acted as a double check.

Sanjay was very discreet and observed almost everything without being obtrusive and his reports matched those of the informants but neither he nor the informants were any match to the shadow who was silently following Sapna everywhere.

Then the fateful day arrived. Sapna and Suresh reached their usual joint, got down at the main entrance and as they entered the cafe, Sanjay swung into the lane and parked the car close to the side entrance from where the young lovers would emerge. They had no sense of time and sometimes spent hours. So after parking the car at the usual place, Sanjay walked briskly down the lane for a quick bite and a cup of tea, he couldn't do without.

Inside the café, Suresh suddenly felt ill and rushed to the wash room. The shadow immediately alerted the snatch team to get to the side entrance. As Suresh came out of the wash room, Sapna saw that he was really sick. She rushed to him in anxiety. He took a glass from the nearest table and gulped some water and felt a little better. She said 'let's go' and started moving towards the side entrance with Suresh leaning on to her for support.

As they emerged from the side entrance, Suresh was hit on the head and he immediately collapsed. Sapna felt a sharp prick in the neck and before she could realize what was happening, her legs felt wobbly and felt someone holding her and hauling her up and then everything went black. No sooner were they thrown into the delivery van standing at the side entrance, than it moved swiftly to the main road and vanished. No one had seen anything.

As Sanjay left the tea shop and started moving towards his car, he saw a yellow delivery van swiftly turning onto the main road. Something about it struck him as strange and made him uneasy. He quickly ran down the lane, rushed into the café and when he didn't find the girl and the boy at their usual table, he frantically looked around but could find them nowhere. His quick enquiries revealed that the boy became ill and that they had left immediately without ordering anything. He feared the worst had happened.

Wasting no time, he ran back to the car and within seconds was racing it to the main road. He swung the car to the right and sped away trying to catch up with the yellow delivery van which was nowhere in sight.

The shadow immediately alerted the team with just two words 'switch fast'. He knew Sanjay would catch up with the van soon and that the whole area would soon be swarming with police and their sniffer dogs. So he quietly moved away to a vantage point from where he could observe unnoticed.

Rao, who was always prepared for the worst, instantly swung into action the moment Sanjay reported the snatch. All roads leading out of the area were immediately barricaded and every vehicle checked. All exit points were put on high alert. The railway police, highway patrol and airport authorities were alerted. Teams from the crime branch were pulled in and dispatched to cover all the exit routes. He himself rushed to the café from where his dear child was abducted. Though seething with rage inside, he maintained a calm demeanor. En-route, he called the informant. Unfortunately, he had seen nothing.

He reached the spot and was happy to see that there was no disruption to normal life and traffic and his men in plain clothes had already zeroed in on the spot. They had quickly reconstructed the event and narrated the same to him. Jacky, the veteran German shepherd was already on the trail and was rearing to go. Realizing there was nothing much to do there for the moment he left the scene following Jacky. The shadow knew that the DCP would come back for missing clues. So he had to find and erase them before he returned. So he went back to the café to look for them and any possible leads the DCP might get when he returned.

Sanjay had meanwhile located the van in one of the by lanes not very far from the café. It lay abandoned and his enquiries revealed nothing. Nobody had seen anything. In fact the lane was hardly frequented and wore a desolate look.

He immediately alerted the DCP and the team descended on the scene soon. Clearly they had switched vehicles here. It seemed they had reached a dead end. The sleuths examined the van which bore the number plate AP 20 T 1405 thoroughly. Except for a small pool of blood, there was nothing else to go by.

The vehicle was traced to one B.K Sarma, proprietor of a small transport business. He was surprised to learn that his vehicle had been stolen. The driver Appulu had left the vehicle at the usual parking slot at about 3 p.m and was with the proprietor in the office located in the cross lane. This was not far from the café. They were both picked up for questioning, anyway. The vehicle was seized and sent for examination.

Sanjay too was taken into custody. He knew it only too well and readily cooperated with the team led by ACP Rathode, a big, burly, bully.

There was no news from the highways or from any of the exit points which meant that they might have crossed the border right under the noses of the patrol forces. The problem was there was nothing to go by. The police didn't have any description or clue. So it was a needle in a haystack situation.

DCP Rao realized that it was not the work of any of the local gangs. Someone big had done it without local help. It was done so clinically and professionally that even the local underworld was still unaware of it even 2 hours after the abduction. So he had to look and think beyond. He closed his eyes and dug into the past to see who could have done it.

Nandini walked in and sat silently opposite watching him. He did not open his eyes but she knew that he was aware of her presence in the room. She had the gift of putting herself in others' shoes to see what they thought.

So, when he opened his eyes and looked at her, she said, "you think it is Rana, right?" He nodded in silence. If it was, then they knew that they were up against a wall. He was never caught because he employed highly efficient professionals who covered their tracks well.

Nandini had felt for some time that they were being followed and had told her husband about it. Knowing her well, he had not ignored her hunch and had put his best men to check. They had drawn a blank. She said, "So, my hunch was right but it was Sapna all the time. My poor girl! Hope she is not hurt." As she said so, she could not hold back the tears. Recovering her composure, she said, "We should inform them." He nodded again. She continued, "Wonder how they will take it. Hope the boy is safe."

"Come in, Sanjay," said Rao. He came in and stood with his head lowered. He knew how they felt and what they were going through. He would probably have felt better if they had shouted and screamed at him. Their silence was oppressive but he also knew that they were very tough and were very composed. So he stood there waiting for them to say something.

"Have you given your statement?" asked Rao. "Yes sir," replied Sanjay.

"Anything you haven't told me?" "No, sir"

"Mr. Saxena," said Nandini. She had always called him by his first name. "Yes, madam," he said.

"We trusted you so much…," she said. "I can never forgive myself for what happened. I am sorry, madam," said Sanjay. There was a dense silence after that as none of them spoke. Rao broke the silence.

"You are not to leave town, right?" said Rao. "Yes sir, I know," replied Sanjay.

"See me tomorrow," said Rao. "Yes sir, but I have no moral right to continue, Sir," replied Sanjay. Rao just nodded his head and looked at Nandini. Taking the cue, she addressed Sanjay and said, "Thank you" by way of dismissal. He left as quietly as he had come in.

They sat in silence lost in their thoughts of their dear darling daughter. The phone rang shrilly jolting them back to the present. He answered mostly in monosyllables and hung up. "The boy is hurt. It was his blood in the van," he said.

"That's bad news. We should tell his parents ourselves, let's go," she said and got up. Remaining seated, he said, "Do I need…" She cut him short and said, "Yes." He was never good at these social responsibilities. It was her forte. He didn't have to worry about that, yet, he reluctantly got up.

It was raining outside now. The whole day had been dull, cloudy and oppressively stuffy. The rain was a relief. While they were on the way to the boy's house, Sanjay was heading towards the café.

Chapter 3

FIRST BREAK

Monday; May 25, 2009

Cuttack

Bikram was cursing the cyclone and the heavy rains that had been lashing the city for the last 4 days. He hadn't ventured out in the last 2 days and was worried what his boss would say if he showed up before him. His boss was very angry with Bikram for having lost his brand new red Honda CRV four days back and had told him never to show his face again. Bikram knew that his boss didn't mean it when he said so. He was just very angry and rightly so. Bikram thought that if he had been the boss he would probably have got his driver arrested and put behind bars. He thought he should be grateful to his boss for being kind to him. It was 2.00 p.m and Bikram thought this was the right time to show up before his boss when he would be relaxing chewing pan after a heavy lunch. So, taking his umbrella out, he stepped out of the house.

As he came out of the house, he froze in astonishment and dropped the umbrella. He couldn't believe his eyes because the car which had gone missing was back in the same place as if it had never gone missing. He fumbled in his pockets and found that he was still carrying the keys.

He rushed to the car and found that there was no visible damage to it. Bikram, nearing 50 was a seasoned driver and a veteran who had seen the world. He knew better than to touch the car. He ran the few streets to his sahib's house. Pattanayak, who was standing in the verandah and wondering when the cyclone would ease, saw Bikram and wondered what bad news the fellow was bringing now. Three days back he had come running like this in the pouring rain to say that his car had vanished. Totally drenched and panting like a dog, he stood there unable to speak which only added to Pattanayak's anxiety. Regaining his breath he told him how miraculously the car has reappeared at the same spot from where it had vanished. Pattanayak thought Bikram had gone mad and was talking nonsense and said so to him.

Nevertheless, he took out his umbrella and followed Bikram who was almost running. When at last they reached the spot, Pattanayak too stood motionless as had Bikram when he first saw it. It was his prized possession and its loss had left him crestfallen. He had never imagined that he would get it back intact. He was so elated and thrilled that he felt like hugging and caressing it but was sane enough to remember that he had lodged a police complaint and that he had to inform them before even touching the car.

So he told Bikram to hang on there and keep an eye lest it should vanish again and rushed to the police station. It was nearly 5.00 p.m and still there was no trace of his boss or the police and that worried Bikram. After some time he felt relieved to see his boss coming followed by a small police team led by the Inspector Agneya Tripathy, of whom Bikram was very scared. The police too were puzzled and confused and stood there unmindful of the heavy rains discussing how it could have happened. They even suspected Bikram of some foul play and questioned him. Luckily for him, his boss came to his rescue and said that Bikram was not intelligent enough to do such things. Finally they said nothing could be done till the morning as they had to follow procedures and formalities before releasing the vehicle. So they posted a constable to keep watch with the strict instruction to see that no one including himself touched the car.

Inspector Tripathy had acted immediately on his return to the Thana. He asked his staff to wait outside when he made a call to Alok Mahapatra, IPS the DCP (Crime). As the gruff voice came on the line, Tripathy said, "Sir, Agnesh from P4 reporting," and waited. "Go on," said the DC. The Inspector narrated the whole story of the missing car and its strange reappearance after 4 days. After hearing him out patiently, he said, "Agnesh this could be serious, do you understand." "Yes, Sir," said Agnesh. He continued, "Good, get the forensic guys, sniffer dogs…you know what to do. See that they are there first thing in the morning. Have it towed to the station first. I don't want any publicity. Ask the owner and the driver to keep their mouths shut. If you think it necessary take them into custody now. I will see you in the morning. If there is anything else, call me whatever be the time." "Yes, Sir," said the Inspector and waited for the call to end.

He then sent a constable to bring Bikram to the station and sent another to ask Pattanayak to call him.

Pattanayak could not sleep that night. Though at first he was very happy about having got back the car so miraculously, he was worried by what the inspector had told him over the phone when he had called as bid by him. The Inspector had asked him not to breathe a word about the car to anyone and said that it looked like the work of highly professional criminals and that it was possible that the car might have been used for committing some crime. So the police would look for finger prints and other clues for any criminal activity and that the vehicle would be released only after thorough examination. If it was suspected that the car had been used in some criminal activity, there would be court proceedings too and the police would expect his cooperation. The last part worried him the most.

Alok then called his counterpart and friend Rao and briefed him about the stolen car and its return. He said, "This could be unconnected but let us not leave any stone unturned. This could very well be the break we are looking for. Let the storm pass tonight. We will start first thing in the morning. Don't worry Rao, we will get them soon. "Thank you, Alok," said Rao, and continued, "Hope it is not too late."

"Hope not. No calls for ransom, yet?" asked Alok. "No. That is what worries me. Nobody has claimed responsibility nor made any demands. So what are they up to?" replied Rao." Let's hope we get the break tomorrow" said Alok, and bidding him good night hung up.

Rao said to Nandini, "I think we have the car they used for the getaway. But where are they?" The question hung in the air.

"Why did the boy suddenly become sick?" Pondered Rao aloud and immediately swung into action as a thought struck him. He jumped out of his seat, called the servant and asked if Sanjay was around. He was and he appeared before him in no time. He was waiting to do something. He told Sanjay to go back to the café and find out if Suresh had taken water before becoming sick and who had served him the glass of water. Sanjay wasted no time and rushed off to the café before they closed at 11.00 p.m.

"That could be the break," said Rao. Nandini agreed and said, "You better catch some sleep."

Chapter 4

CALM AFTER STORM

Tuesday; May 26, 2009

Kolkata

Premnath woke up with a start. The clock showed 6.20. The rain had stopped. The morning was still quiet. He wondered what had woken him up. He felt wide awake yet did not feel like getting out of bed. So he lay there with eyes open and thoughts drifting back to his childhood. He remembered how his father would wake him up by 6.30, help him with the toilet and then bathe him. He would then bring him a glass of milk with lots of sugar in it and watch him drink it. He would then bring him his books. Premnath would study sincerely for an hour by which time his father would get ready to leave for work.

His mother was lazy and would wake up only by about 8.00. She was a foul mouthed alcoholic who drove both the father and son crazy. But his father, being a good man was still good to her because she had gotten him such a sweet son.

Premnath was by now nearly 8 years old and was doing very well in his studies making his father proud. Life was good despite his mother and her tantrums. As they say good things don't last long.

It happened one day. He returned from school and as he turned into the lane, he found a crowd in front of his house. He rushed home and saw his mother sitting crestfallen surrounded by several women of the neighbourhood speaking to her in hushed tones. Sensing something was wrong, he ran to her. The moment she saw him, she hugged him and started crying inconsolably. He didn't understand why she was crying but couldn't control himself. He started crying too. They told him that his father was dead.

He didn't understand what it meant until he saw the body they brought home. Seeing the inert body of his father he understood what it meant to be dead. He cried over the body and pleaded to his father to get up. He cried and cried till his eyes dried up.

They made him burn his father's body. He screamed that he wouldn't but ultimately he did after the Dadu (old man), their next door neighbor told him that only if he did as told would his father's soul reach the abode of Gods and that he would bless him and protect him from the skies like a guiding star. Yet, he was so worked up that if they had not held him back, he would have jumped into the burning pyre.

That was the end of his school and education. His uncle took over the family affairs and drove him to work and bring home money. He made it clear 'no money, no food.' His mother joined his uncle and beat him if he didn't bring home any money. Life became hell. He missed his father and cried every night looking for him in the skies.

With a sudden jolt, he came back to the present. It was nearing 9.00 a.m. It was warm and sunny. The storm had passed. He wondered what had woken him up again. He got up and became busy with washing, cleaning, bathing and cooking. By about 11.00, the smell of hot food made him hungry. So he sat down to take a leisurely meal.

Across the street, Sardari Begum, generally called 'badi ammi' was sitting on her regal bed like a queen holding a durbar with three boys seated before her. They had introduced themselves to her as Veeru, Vijay and Vikram students of Jadavpur University doing their masters degree in Sociology. They were here to see her in connection with their research project titled "How Golden is the Golden Tree?" – A Study on the life of the sex workers of Sonagachi, the largest such district in Asia.

When asked what they intended to achieve through the Study, they had replied that they wanted to bring about a social change in the perception of the lives of the sex workers, especially among the youth, so that they develop a positive attitude towards sex workers and their children.

The purpose of their visit was to understand firsthand the magnitude of the trade, socio, economic and political environment in which the trade functioned, living and health conditions of the workers, social issues faced by the children of the workers and what the future held for them and so on.

Appreciating their objective and seriousness, the Begum, who was still strikingly beautiful, said, "The name Sonagachi has really nothing to do with the trade, though it has come to be associated with it over time. The place derived its name from the Sufi Saint Sonar Ghazi whose Dargah is located here. With over 10,000 workers doing business in the area, the distorted and localized name has become popular. So there is nothing golden about the place. But with the ever growing number of workers, over the years the trade has grown like a large banyan tree fanning out and sheltering all those who take refuge under it. There is no need to change the title of your project. Let it remain. It's good."

She continued, "The system works like this. As in everything else, service is directly related to the social and economic status of the customer. The upper class and the rich are catered to by Class A workers who charge amounts varying from Rs. 8,000 to Rs. 12,000 an hour. They do not go out and so have to depend on pimps or agents to bring customers to them. About 50% of it goes to their mistresses or towards renting a room. The agent gets a share of the remaining. The agents also charge about 25% separately from the customers. Class B workers charge about half of what the Class A girls do and operate on their own either through their regular clientele or by taking to the streets.

The rent for a high end room is anywhere between Rs. 10,000 to 15,000 a month. Under the contract system a room can be hired by upto 3 workers. When the landlords cannot hike the rent, they collect charges for facilities like television for which they collect additional charges ranging from Rs. 800 to 1,200 a month.

Girls who cater to the middle class and the lower class charge a minimum of Rs. 500 an hour and for regular clientele they may even offer a discount of Rs. 100. The actual charges depend on factors like whether the client wants a cot with mattress or just a mat on the floor."

Veeru interrupted her to ask whether the economic slowdown has affected the trade here.

"Definitely," said the Begum, "the world's oldest profession is no exception. Many Class A workers have had to either slash their rates or become Class B workers. What can they do when they get only 3 customers a night as against a minimum of 5 they used to get earlier. With Real Estate rates spiraling landlords too have increased the room rents. With new girls coming in all the time, there is competition for space. Discounts have also become more common. So like everyone else in business, we are also going through hard times."

Vijay chipped in with the query, "So how do they manage?" "There is only one way," replied the Begum, "we have to work harder and not lose hope. But as long as there are men in the city, we women are in business." Saying so, she gave a hearty laugh.

It was Vikram who spoke now. "How did you get into this, madam?" he asked.

'I was born in 1971 in Punji, a small tribal village in a far off district of Bangladesh. They say I was as beautiful as wild flowers of the hills and named me Choto Shaluk.' "Isn't that a Hindu name?" queried Vikram.

"No. Shaluk[2] is the name of a blue water lily, a very beautiful flower. Interestingly, I was born a Hindu but circumstances made me a Muslim. It doesn't really matter. What matters is that I am a woman, a doll anybody could play around with. When I was about 5 years old, my mother died when she gave birth to my sister. Being a weakling she didn't survive. She too died within three days. So while my father went out and worked, I looked after the household chores – from cooking to everything. Soon, my father married another woman and from a daughter, I became a servant. When my step mother gave birth to a son, I became his ayah too. By the time I became 10, there were two more kids. I was a full fledged house keeper and was fully stretched to the limit of breaking down.

---

2 Shaluk, *Nymphaeastellata* also called Neel Padma, Neel Sapla, Sundi. Flowers solitary, 7.5–15 cm diam., pale violet, less commonly light blue or purple; petals oblong to oblong-lanceolate.

One of the plantation workers, a friend of my mother, had stopped visiting us after my father re-married. She knew my plight and had a lot of sympathy for me. She was my only well wisher. The others in the village hardly cared. One day she met me and told me that one of her relatives was visiting them and that he would be leaving for Dhaka in a couple of days. She had spoken to him about me and had asked him to do something for me. He had told her that I could go with him to Dhaka where he could find me a place to live and work. They knew that my father would never agree and would stop me if he even got a hint of this suggestion. The only option for me was to run away.

Being a small tribal village, if we left together, the whole village will know sooner or later and my well wisher would be in trouble. So it was decided that he would go ahead and wait for me at Sirimongol. The next day I would follow. He would meet me at Sirimongol and take me to Dhaka from there. The plan scared me and left me sleepless. The lure of freedom from the slavery was too strong and I took the bold step and told her 'Yes'.

When the day came, I fled. When I arrived at Sirimongol and found him waiting at the Bus Station, I felt relieved and all the fears and anxieties I suffered during the journey vanished. He took me to a hotel and bought me lunch. We then left for Dhaka."

"How old was he?" enquired Veeru.

"He must have been about 24 or 25 not more, though I am not sure. In fact I don't even know his name. He was called Bappi, I know only that much about him," replied the Begum and continued her story.

"Dhaka was a huge city compared to the small village, the only world I had known till then. I was overwhelmed and scared. The first thing he did was change my name and religion. He said I would be safer that way because if my father reported to the police, they would be looking for a missing Hindu tribal girl. It made sense and so I agreed. He took me to an old man who had started a garment business and was employing young girls. The man said I was too young to be legally employed. When he asked my name, Bappi said 'Sardari Begum'. He told him that during the liberation, I had lost my parents and since then he had been supporting me. The old man took pity, as he himself had lost his family during the war. He said I could work there as a helper and live with the girls in the dormitory. I never saw Bappi again in my life. He had come as an angel from the heavens to save me from the slavery of my own home. He was truly God sent.

Almost all the girls who worked there were Muslims. Most of them were local residents who came to work from their homes. Some outstation girls lived in the dormitory. Though they initially shunned me, they soon came to like me very much after seeing how useful I was to them. In a way I became indispensable.

When I came of age, I was lucky that I was among such girls who were more than sisters to me. So the transition was not traumatic or scary. Soon I became the darling of my sisters. They were also very scared for me because of my striking beauty.

Then as fate would have it, the old man died and some nephew of the old man, Nazrul Hassan inherited the business. He was working in Kolkata. So he gave the business on lease to a local businessman who said he could not keep me in employment as I was still a minor and that he would face problems with the police and government authorities.

Nazrul told him not to worry as he had decided to take me with him to Kolkata. I didn't want to leave the comfort of this home where I had found love, kindness and care. I wept and wept. The girls then told me that Nazrul had fallen head over heels in love with me and that I should make the most of it. They understood the inescapable position I was in.

It took him about 3 weeks to get my papers ready. So in 1985, I landed in Kolkata. Nazrul straightaway brought me to this house and lodged me here with the old woman who was running the brothel. I was given a separate room and kept away from the other girls. The next night, Nazrul came to my room and spoke to me. He said he was married and had a family. He then told me that he owned this house and was its landlord. The old woman was a mistress who ran the brothel here. When I started crying, he said nobody would touch me except him. He said I was his second wife so I was not to mess around with other men. If I did, his goons would kill me.

So started my sex life. The girls, my Dhaka sisters had already prepared me for it. He visited me thrice a week and I lived like a queen because everybody treated me with respect. Life was not bad. I didn't even know how 5 years had passed.

Then one fine Sunday morning, the old woman who ran the brothel here died. Nazrul came promptly and attended to all the arrangements for her funeral. In the evening he called the girls who were working under the old woman and told them that from then on I was the mistress of the place. He then gave them the choice of either working under me or going on their own. They chose to remain. Since I knew nothing of the trade, he called his right hand man Shamim and told him to assist me in learning the ropes. So even before turning 20, I had become a mistress."

"You were lucky in a way," remarked Veeru. She laughed and said, "Yes, you can say that." "Why do they call you 'badi ammi'?" asked Vijay.

"The girls, who called the old woman 'badi ammi', started calling me the same as they didn't know what else to call me."

"Are those girls still here?" asked Vijay. "No, except for one," replied the Begum, "but there are others. Everyday new girls keep coming into this world."

"Shamim is also a procurer and that keeps the house full. He gets only Class A girls."

"Is there any new girl we can meet?" asked Vikram. "No. Sorry, you can't meet any of the girls," said the Begum firmly.

Suddenly, they all felt cold and a strange sense of fear gripped them.

Vijay immediately changed the topic and asked the Begum about police harassment. She laughed and said that they did their 'duty' now and then. They would raid the place and file a report after taking their pound of flesh – both literally and symbolically. They never arrested or touched the girls or the pimps. It was always the customers they caught and extracted whatever they could from them too.

"What about the media and the social workers, NGOs?" asked Vikram.

"Everyone is in it for money. They all do their bit and in the end nothing happens. Nobody wants anything to change. Even documentaries and films have been made about us and Sonagachi. We get some publicity. The politicians immediately make use of it to serve their own ends and get some publicity for themselves. Soon everyone forgets and business goes on as usual."

"What about health workers?" asked Veeru. "In what way are they different?" asked the Begum in reply.

"What about HIV? Are the workers protected?" Veeru didn't want to give up.

"I can say we take all precautions and there is no case of infection. But then the truth is that like anywhere else, about 50% are affected," replied the Begum.

"Don't the workers insist on the use of condoms?" continued Veeru.

"Yes, they do in their own interest. But the customers don't feel comfortable or happy. So they even pay 25% extra for not using the condom. How can we deny them that when that is what they come here for – satisfaction?" replied the Begum.

"Isn't it paradoxical?" asked Vijay and continued, "on the one hand people come here to quench their lust and wash their sins, and on the other hand come here to take *punya mati* from *nishbhidho palli* as an essential ingredient in making the idols of Ma Durga during the Puja. Why do they do it?"

"It is not," replied the Begum, "the belief is that man loses his virtues here when he becomes a slave to his lust and the woman binds herself in shackles to be his courtesan and slaves to satisfy his lust. Both lose their virtues here making the *mati* pure or virtuous. So the priests and potters come here begging us for a bag of this soil."

"Wasn't there a problem last year when women here refused to entertain such requests?" asked Vijay.

"Yes, there was; but in the end they gave in because the business men smelt an opportunity and started selling the *punya mati* for a price. That is because people still believe in the tradition and even doubt that an idol may have been made without using the *punya mati*. So, in most pandals, the priests dip their hands in a bowl of this soil and smear it on the idol before starting the Puja."

"What do you think?" asked Vijay.

She laughed and said, "What do I think? Well, everyone has a right to his opinion. A woman can become a mother only if she consummates. A mother is a mother. It doesn't matter whether she is a pativrata or a prostitute. There is nothing unholy about mating. Every mother does. Otherwise you and I would not have been born. I would call this a place of worship of *Kama*, an essential part of life. If people consider this place and its soil holy even if it is only during the Puja, so what's wrong in that?

Now we celebrate Puja here like any other place, though there was lot of resistance to it when we started. The *pandal* is now visited by thousands of people. We even have *sindur khela*, you know?"

Changing the track abruptly, Vikram asked, "Where can we find Nazrul? Can we meet him?"

"You will have to die to meet him," she said laughing aloud, "he died a long time ago and left me this house, some amount of money and the garment business in Dhaka. Since I had no intention of going back there, I gave it to a cooperative society formed by my sisters working there. The least I could do for them was that."

"How did you manage after that?" asked Vikram.

"Simple. Everyone looked up to me to continue in his place. They made me an automatic successor and boss. Being a total illiterate, I knew nothing about finance, but I understood money. Shamim is a total loyalist and a shrewd business man like Nazrul. He arranged for some select high end clients for me who would pay a very handsome fee."

"Do you take from the girls working for you the same 50% you mentioned earlier?" asked Veeru.

She skirted the question and answered, "Nothing comes for free in this world. It takes care of their food, shelter, clothing they get from here. It also gives them the freedom to leave if they want."

Just then they heard a lot of noise from inside and a girl rushed in huffing and puffing and said breathlessly, "Badi ammi, it is Shibani again. God knows what has come over her this morning. Can you please come?"

The Begum quickly and gracefully rose from her bed and dismissed the boys with a wave of her hand. The boys too got up and started saying something but found themselves facing three muscular men. Feeling intimidated and scared, the boys backed out and left the house in a hurry. The interview had come to an abrupt end unceremoniously.

They almost tumbled out of the house. It was nearing 1.00 and they felt hungry. The thought of life behind those doors made their throats feel dry. Finding the street deserted and the shops opposite still closed, they headed towards Chittaranjan Avenue.

Chapter 5

STRANGE HAPPENINGS

Tuesday; May 26, 2009

Kolkata

Post lunch Premnath relaxed for an hour and after doing the utensils and necessary preparations, opened the shop around 1.00 p.m. The road still looked deserted and desolate in the aftermath of the storm. He put the benches outside and waited for a customer to begin the day's business. Premnath had learnt that patience always paid.

The adjoining workshops were still closed and so the usual activities and the demand for tea and snacks were missing. Life seemed to be returning to normal across the street too. The girls had started coming out to sit on the stairs or stand in the doorways hoping to catch a day customer. The fragrance of talcum and perfumes drifted across and hung in the air. He felt no sympathy or compassion for them probably because of his hatred towards women but he did not loathe them. After all, his business flourished only because of them. Men who came for them brought him his business. They were in the same boat depending on the same customer for their livelihood.

As he sat there for hours with no sight of a customer yet, he had a strange feeling that he was not alone. As it started getting dark, business started ticking slowly. It was still dull and Premnath, like the girls across the street, hoped it would pick up as the night progressed. The pimps had now joined the girls and taken up their positions. He didn't care for them either and hated them as they reminded him of his uncle. They had sensed it long ago and ignored him. It suited him fine as he didn't want any of their gossips from their filthy mouths.

Some of the usual customers showed up and as had become customary sat there sipping their tea before making up their minds on choosing the girl for the night. They talked about the storm and the deaths it had caused before moving on with the paan of their choice in the mouth. Some of them would sit there, and chew their paan before making their moves. He had seen all sorts of characters which made him realize that it takes all sorts to make a world. Each one created a business for the other, thought Premnath philosophically.

It was past 9.00 p.m and business had picked up somewhat. One of the regular customers who always sought a new girl every time came and sat at his usual place on the bench. After his quota of tea, cigarette and paan, he was preparing to leave. Though he knew that Premnath didn't talk girls, he asked him if there was something new. Then as he moved, he tripped and fell flat face down. As he was falling he hit the bench. Premnath rushed out of his shop and lifted him up. The fellow was badly hurt and was bleeding from the nose but luckily he was conscious. A pimp from across had joined in by then. He hailed a taxi, put the fellow in and dispatched him asking the driver to take him to the nearest clinic or wherever he wanted to go.

Premnath was disturbed by the incident. It was not good for his business. He looked around to see what had caused the man to triplike that but could find no clues. He cleaned the bench and sat there puzzled. Suddenly he had the same strange feeling that he was not alone. But there was no one except him. Feeling uneasy, he went back into the shop to wait for the next customer.

The pimp who had gone back to his position also wondered how someone could fall like that. It seemed as though somebody had tripped him. But then there was no one except the man. Even the shop keeper was inside. He knew the customer. He was a regular who asked for a new girl every time. There were some new comers he could have offered the man. Bad luck, he thought. Suddenly he felt very chill and a little feverish. He cursed the weather and rushed in pushing aside the girls who wondered what was wrong with him. The night wore on without further 'incidents'.

Elsewhere, Ranjit Mullick continued to be grilled by the police of the Kidderpore PS. He told them for the hundredth time that he had gone to his village to see his ailing mother only with the permission of his employer. The container truck he normally drove was parked at the usual place when he had left. He had given the keys to his employer after parking the vehicle and it was still with the employer. He pleaded that he had not stolen the vehicle. He was not even aware that it had been stolen.

The police wouldn't listen. They kept beating him and asking where he had hidden the vehicle or whether he had sold it. Inspector Bijoy Dasgupta was a ruthless cop who specialized in extracting statements through merciless treatment of suspects. So he would quickly gauge if a suspect was telling lies or the truth. He knew Ranjit was telling him the truth. He had seen the train tickets when they had searched his place after picking him up. But he still kept the pressure on in the hope that he might give him some lead knowingly or unknowingly. Just then a constable appeared and told him that there was a call from the Highway Patrol. To Ranjit's relief, the Inspector left to take the call.

As expected by Inspector Dasgupta, it was about the stolen truck. The truck lay abandoned on NH6 in the Lodhasuli Forest area. He immediately informed the crime branch who had asked him to alert them instantly if any stolen vehicle was found. Dasgupta was now convinced that Ranjit was innocent. He felt that the matter was far too big and rotten.

He felt sorry that he had beaten the hell out of the poor chap. But it was his duty to suspect and to treat suspects like that. He didn't know any other way. He always felt miserable after knowing that he had beaten up an innocent man and tried to make amends. So he came back to the cell. Ranjit cringed on seeing him return. The Inspector pulled up a chair, sat down and called the Constable. He told him to get some bread, biscuits and tea for Ranjit. When he was gone, he said, "Sorry, I was only doing my duty. Forgive me." Ranjit thought that the Inspector was preparing him for another bout of beatings and frantically waved his hands and tried to say, 'please let me go.' No words came out as his throat was totally dry.

Dasgupta understood what the fellow was saying and gesturing to him to calm down, said, "it is very late in the night now. Have some tea and bread. Then you can sleep here and leave in the morning." Ranjit didn't know whether or not to believe him. So he just cupped his hands in prayer.

The inspector left abruptly. The constable too showed some compassion when he brought him some bread and tea. He then threw a blanket at Ranjit and left him to his peace. Though every inch of his body ached, he fell asleep soon. It appeared that the bread and tea did the trick. He didn't know that the tea was drugged to help him sleep.

The lone constable on NH6 who was assigned to guard the abandoned truck was feeling cold and listless. He was scared of spirits and he didn't know what spirits lay waiting for him in this Godforsaken forest. He cursed the fellow who chose to abandon the vehicle here and the Inspector who chose him to guard the cursed vehicle. Normally there would be a constant flow of vehicles on the highway but because of the storm, the Highway lay deserted.

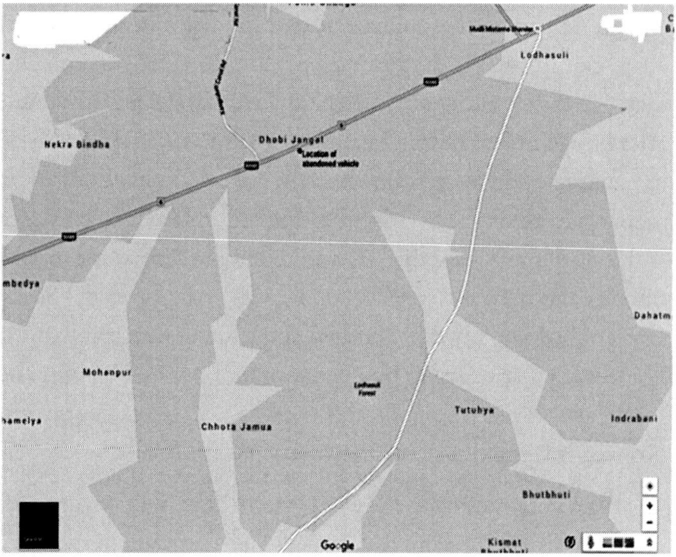

Though the storm had passed, traffic was yet to pick up. Only a stray vehicle passed once in a while. So he cursed the storm too. He felt like taking refuge inside the cabin of the abandoned truck but he had been clearly instructed to stay clear of it. In a way it was good because the cursed truck lay inside the thick vegetation hidden from view. He thought he was better off on the highway where he could stop the passing vehicles and in the guise of checking papers could be in touch with living humans. So he sat there on his bike dozing in fits and jumping at every sound of which there was no dearth.

In an undisclosed location, Rana Randhir Singh a.k.a Rana was staring at the two men before him. His prolonged silence and piercing stare was killing them.

He then turned and looked at Bablu, the man in charge of this operation. "Why did they have to kill the boy? What a waste. Do you know how much he would have fetched? I had such wonderful plans. Pssss…, all the plans have gone up into thin air. Why? all because some idiot chose to use his thick head instead of just following instructions."

Bablu was glaring at the two men. He was seething with rage and was ready to tear them apart.

Rana turned to the two men. They immediately fell at his feet and started pleading for mercy. He showed his annoyance and waved them to get out of his sight. They were confused and scared. Fearing the worst to follow, they left the room and waited in the outer verandah.

Rana gave Bablu, 'you know what to do' look. Bablu nodded and before he could leave, Rana said, "And don't forget to inform DCP Rao."

Back in Hyderabad, Rao had received information of the abandoned truck. He was almost certain that it had everything to do with his daughter's abduction. It was becoming clearer as to how the abduction must have been carried out. Events were unfolding. He needed faces now. He had immediately called his team and summoned them to his house by 8.00 the following morning for a review and to chalk out an action plan which was already emerging in his mind. So he too didn't sleep well.

Chapter 6

TURN OF EVENTS

Wednesday; May 27, 2009

Hyderabad

The meeting started at 8.00 sharp. The team had assembled by 7.45 itself.

After deliberating on all the information gathered, Krishna Kumar, IPS, the ACP and the right hand of Rao reconstructed the events and presented the picture that emerged.

The victims were under close surveillance by a highly professional gang and the abduction was carried out after meticulous planning. Suresh Babu on entering the café always drank a glass of water. So they tampered with it to make him instantly sick.

"Do we know what was used?" asked one of the senior inspectors. "Yes, apomorphine hydrochloride. It is an emetic, something that is used in rat poison so that if someone consumes the poison, it gets expelled from the body before absorption. It causes instant nausea and induces vomiting almost immediately. Heavier doses can even be harmful.

We do not as yet know for certain who administered it and how, though we are pursuing some clues we got. That is a gap we need to fill."

"Please continue," said Rao.

"The delivery van waiting in readiness was moved to the side entrance immediately on being alerted and grabbed them as they came out of the café. There must have been two powerful people. Otherwise they could not have moved so fast. Also they must have drugged them to knock them out instantly. It could have been morphine (yet to be confirmed). There was a third at the wheel to move the van swiftly out of the doorway before anyone noticed anything. They took the van to the alley where it was found and transferred the victims to the Honda CRV stolen from Cuttack. Their cell phones crushed beyond use were found at the site.

The Honda did not leave the city on its own wheels. It was stuffed into a 40' container and so safely crossed the border without raising suspicion. There must have been another car or SUV inside the container. The victims were transferred into that vehicle and the Honda was driven back into Cuttack and returned to the place from where it was stolen. This must have been done just outside Cuttack at some appointed place. Probably, it was picked up from the same spot."

"Can you elaborate on that, Sir?" asked another official.

"Our understanding is like this. They must have used some local thief to steal the car and leave it at a particular place, and come back and take it at an appointed date and time and put it back from where he stole it. That way when he was caught, he would know nothing about the actual purpose for which the car was used."

"Has anyone been caught?" was the next question.

The ACP answered, "Local police have picked up three suspects and are questioning them. At best we may get a name or a description of the guy who paid him handsome money to do the job and to keep his mouth shut. It is almost certain that it may not lead us anywhere. Nevertheless we shall follow it to its logical end."

Then he continued, "The container truck then took the roundabout route NH6 and after entering West Bengal, the truck was abandoned in the forest and the culprits left by the other vehicle with the boy and the girl. Which way they headed from there is as yet unclear. The regular driver of the truck Ranjit was apparently on leave and away from Kolkata when the truck was stolen and he returned to Kolkata before it resurfaced. For now, it appears that he is innocent. He has been released but is being shadowed. We will be alerted if a contact is made."

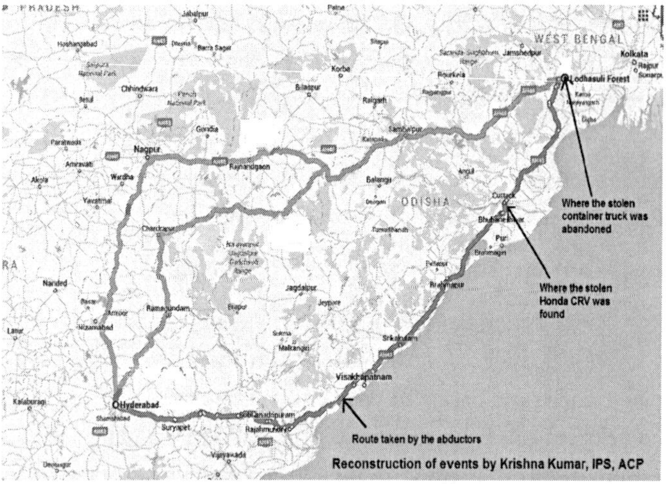

"So what is the action plan, Sir?"

Now the DCP answered, "Let us check all the check posts and toll plazas and check when the truck passed them; find out who were on duty at the posts and elicit a description of the driver. We may get more than one description, doesn't matter. It may even be better that way as we get more than one lead.

They may have crossed several borders by now and may be holed up somewhere. Let us flush the rats out of their holes. The ACP has already drawn up the plans. Please take briefings from him and leave. I want everyone out in 10 minutes flat. "Good luck" so saying he concluded the meeting that lasted just 15 minutes.

At the breakfast table Rao said to Nandini, "No news yet. Even the local gangs are not aware. It won't be long before media gets wind of it. Then they will be all over the place."

"Then we should leak it to them, don't you think. The publicity may hurt the rascals who did it more than it can hurt us," said Nandini.

"No, no. We are on their trail. The moment we have a face we will know who to go after. Until then let them feel cool. That's when they will make a mistake. I want them to. If things get hot now, they may lie low. It will then become that much more difficult to save Sapna and the boy. You never know what they may do to them. So let's give it a day and see," replied Rao.

Neither ate properly. Though they kept up a calm exterior, they were extremely anxious and disturbed. As they sat with their coffee cups in hand, the land line telephone rang. Before the servant could pick it up, Rao took the call on the extension. Even before he could say hello, the caller said, "Panimeindekh (look in the water)." "Who is it, where are you calling from," asked Rao sharply. There was just silence at the other end and then the line went dead.

"Who was it and what did he say?" asked Nandini. Rao shook his head and said, "He wants us look for them in the water. He wants me to trace this call." He immediately called the control room and asked them to trace the call.

"Water, what does that mean – sea, river, canal, well?" asked Nandini worry written all over her face.

Rao replied, "It could just be a ploy to distract us and send us barking up the wrong tree."

He went on to assure her, "Don't worry. Nothing has happened to our girl. I am sure of that."

The call was traced to Dehri in Aurangabad District of Bihar. He immediately called his counterpart in Bihar and alerted him about the call. The call had originated from a PCO on the Canal Road. The woman sitting at the PCO remembered the man who had made the call because she was surprised that he had spent hardly a minute or so and didn't appear to have even spoken. The man was of small frame, even frail you could say, shabby and hardly the type who made even local calls, leave alone STD calls. He was clad in black shorts and a yellow banian, both faded and dirty. He walked awkwardly limping a little and wore no footwear.

Within 30 minutes he was picked up from the entrance of the Railway Station Dehri on Sone. He turned out to be a rag picker. He said that the previous night when he was lying under the tree half awake and half asleep, a man put a knife to his throat and told him what he wanted him to do. He was then given the phone number and 30 bucks for the call and another 100 bucks for making the call. If he didn't do that or tried to act smart or run away, he would kill him. He didn't want to die, so he had done what he was paid to do. No, he hadn't seen him. He was confused whether it was real or he had been dreaming. When he saw the cash in his hand, he realized it was real. By then there was no one around. He doubted if it was a man or ghost.

No, he didn't know what 'look in the water' meant. He had no clue. He was asked to say that and he had. He knew nothing beyond that.

The Inspector called Rao and briefed him and after about 10 minutes sent two men to the Sone River and two men to the Sone Canal to scout for clues.

The constable guarding the truck on NH 6 was feeling tired and hungry. It was nearing 10.00 a.m and yet there was no sign of any reliever. Just as he was giving up hope, he saw a convoy of police vehicles approaching. He came to immediate attention. No sooner than they arrived, they cordoned off the place, forensic men got to work, the sniffer dogs swung into action and ran into the jungle followed by running policemen. Suddenly the place came alive and became a hub of activities. Nobody seemed to bother or care about the constable who had guarded the truck the whole night in the middle of nowhere. He felt miserable and thought that he should give up this thankless job. He thought he should leave immediately since nobody, not even his immediate boss seemed to be concerned. But he didn't have the guts to do so.

He then heard his boss cry out in pain and a commotion followed. He ran into the jungle in the direction of the commotion. He ran almost half a kilometer. He reached the spot and stood there panting. He found his boss lying on the ground and a man was trying to help him up in vain. There was one more man trying to hold back the dogs which were looking down a deep gorge and were barking away like mad.

"What are you waiting for? Come give me a hand," shouted his boss, a big burly man. The two men helped him up. The 200 pound plus inspector leaned heavily on his subordinate as he rose from the ground with great effort. The constable who was already dead tired and hungry felt that he would break under the weight of his boss. The man had sprained his ankle. So limping heavily and supported by the poor constables he made it to the nearest boulder and sat down on it sweating profusely from the effort. The dogs were getting on his nerves by now. So he asked them what the racket was all about.

The constables joined the dog trainer who was straining to keep the dogs on leash. They looked down and found a body about 20' below in the deep gorge. If it hadn't been for the broken tree trunk the body would have slid deeper down. They returned and reported it to the Inspector who shouted to the trainer to take the dogs back to the vehicle and come back to help him make it back to the highway.

As the noise of the dogs being dragged back died down, the Inspector called his DC and reported the finding of a body in the gorge. Next he alerted the Homicide squad of Kharagpaur district police who would take over the investigation. He then called his friends in the Forest Department and asked them to send a team to assist the police in retrieving the body from the gorge.

It was nearly noon by then. If the Homicide and Forest teams didn't arrive soon, they might have to wait another day to get the body out. Meanwhile the forensic guys were through with their work on the truck. There was not much they could get except that there were distinctly different tyre marks indicating that there had been two vehicles inside the container. Surprisingly there were no finger prints. The vehicle was thoroughly cleansed of all marks except the tyre marks which seemed quite strange.

Chapter 7

CHILLING EVENTS

Wednesday; May 27, 2009

Kolkata

"No," screamed Shibani as Shamim advanced again. She stood blocking a closed door. That brought the Begum and some of the girls to the scene.

Shamim had tried to push her out of the way twice but had failed to move her even an inch. He was puzzled how a frail girl like her could manage to obstruct him so. Normally, she would not even stand before him, so he wondered where she got the courage and strength from. He was going mad with rage. Such things were happening since the previous night. He could not let such nonsense continue. He was determined to put an end to this even if it meant killing the girl. So he advanced furiously.

The moment he put his hand on her, she twisted his to the point of breaking it. No one had ever heard Shamim scream in pain. When he resisted it only got worse. Then she pushed him. He fell a good ten feet away.

The Begum and her girls were too shocked and scared even to look at Shibani. They looked in disbelief at Shamim who was lying still and motionless where he had fallen. Then she said menacingly, "No one goes inside. If you try, you will die. Is that understood?" They all nodded in unison as the cat seemed to have got their tongue.

The Begum was the first to move. She took control of the situation and asked the girls to go and attend to their work. She then helped Shamim up and sent him to his quarters accompanied by a couple of his goons who were too dazed by the incident to do anything.

She then approached Shibani and said, "Come my child, calm down. If you do not want anyone to go in there, no one will." The girl immediately collapsed and fainted. Then she sat there and took the girl's head on her lap and stroked it soothingly. She was the apple of her eye and the Begum loved her like a mother because she was the only one who called her 'Ma' and not 'badi ammi' like the other girls. She was deeply worried but could not afford to show it lest there would be no control and all hell would break loose. She had to keep this matter quiet and under control.

Shibani hailed from a small backward village of Hariharpara in Murshidabad where poverty was a norm. She was fondly called Gudia. Her parents, who struggled to stay alive themselves, were hard pressed to feed their children. They felt they would starve to death. It was then that a man approached them and told them of opportunities for young girls to work as domestic help in Kolkata. He offered them a handsome price for their eldest daughter. It was too good to be refused. Moreover, at least she would have a livelihood instead of dying here in Hariharpara, they thought. So, when she was about 8 years old, she was sold for Rs. 500/-. The man told Shibani that he would take her to the big city where she would be married to a Prince and would live happily. The girl had heard stories of such Princes from her grandmother and innocently believed it to be true. Still when it came to parting, she cried and begged not to be separated from her mother. But she had been sold which fact she did not know. Her mother was torn between the realities of poverty and the emotions of losing her first born and her dearest child. She could not bear to see her go and ran into the hut and cried and cried.

The girl was kept in a house along with other girls, most of whom were elder to her. She thought they were all waiting for their Princes like her. She had been made to believe as such. In fact she had been sold to the mistress of a brothel in Sonagachi for Rs. 5000/-.

After she attained puberty, she was also made to stand along with other girls in a row. She still believed she was going to be chosen by a Prince to be married off to him. The day a customer chose her, reality hit her. She somehow managed to run away from the brothel without knowing where to go. She was picked up by a policeman and taken to the station. There they fed her and gave her a blanket and pillow to sleep in a room. She thought she had done the right thing in approaching the policeman. As night progressed, she woke up to see the policeman standing above her in nothing but only an underwear. She tried to get up and wriggle out but he was too powerful. She was raped by four of them. As the day broke out, they told her to get out. Realizing that there was no place to go to and that she would meet with the same fate wherever she may go, she went back to Sonagachi, but not to the dirty little house owned by the old sack but to the 'big house'. The Begum saw her, heard her story, took pity and brought her up as if she were her own daughter. She told her that she would not be forced into the trade unless and until the day she decided of her own free will to do so. The Begum loved her like a mother. The girl thanked Durga Mai for having given her a loving mother who loved, cared and fed her.

Shibani sat up and was surprised to see her Ma sitting on the floor outside the door of her room. She wanted to know what had happened. 'Nothing,' assured the Begum. The girl was not convinced. She wanted to know why the other girls were avoiding her and even seemed to be scared of her. The Begum assured her that it was the wretched storm that had disrupted business badly putting the girls on edge. Now that it was all over, things would return to normal, she said, and told her not to worry herself too much.

Before Shibani could say anything more, she called out to Rameela, one of the senior girls with a level head on her shoulders, to bring some tea. Rameela appeared almost immediately as if she had been waiting in the wings with the tea. She smiled at Shibani as if nothing had happened and sat by her side after setting the tea tray in front of the Begum. She then poured out the tea into the 3 cups. After passing on the cups to Begum and Shibani she took her own and started sipping the tea. She then went on to tell the Begum what was being prepared for lunch and roped Shibani into the conversation.

The hot tea and the normal calm conversation soothed Shibani's anxieties and soon got her chatting as always. The Begum rose and the girls followed. She said, "Go rest for a while before lunch" and as Shibani began to say something, she said, "Don't worry. Everything will be as you want, I will take care."

The girl said, "My sweet Ma, I love you." Kissing the Begum on the cheek, she went into the room and locked it. Before doing so, she hugged Rameela whom she always adored. Sighing heavily, the Begum said, "Let no one disturb her." Rameela smiled and said, "No one would dare to now, don't worry."

The Begum retired to her room. Rameela followed soon and said, "Badi ammi, I have called the girls who were on the scene. You better talk to them lest they talk to others." Begum looked at the girl admiringly and thought 'what an understanding girl. I don't know what I would do without her.'

The girls came in. There were seven of them. They all looked pale and scared. When she gestured to them to come, they came and sat by her side still shaky and unsure. She said in her soft caressing voice, "I want you girls to be happy and smiling all the time. It pains me to see you girls looking so worried. There is nothing to worry. Everything is fine. As for Shibani, you know how badly laid up she was with fever. Hardly had she recovered and the storm broke out and the fever relapsed. There is no fever now but she is yet to recover her health. The last 15 days have been traumatic for her. So she is still edgy.

Give her some time and she will be her normal self. You continue to talk to her as you did earlier. Don't ignore her. She means no harm to anyone and won't hurt any of you, I assure you. Also as you know, she is a little touchy about her things. So don't go to her room unless she calls you."

They seemed to be confused and still unsure. No one ventured to say anything.

Rameela broke the ice and said, "Look, I had tea with her and we chatted for nearly half an hour. She didn't do anything to me. She even hugged me as usual. If you don't talk to her or if you try to avoid her when she speaks to you, you will only make her feel that there is something wrong. That is not going to help her recover. If her health continues to be bad, badi ammi may also fall ill from worry. Do we want all that?"

"No," they said in one voice, "Nothing should happen to badi ammi."

The Begum assured them, "Nothing will happen to me if we all live normally like a happy family, like we have been living all along."

"I will," said Mithali hugging the Begum. "Me too, me too" cooed the others. Then Mithali said, "Badi ammi, we are sorry we made you unhappy. But after seeing what she did to bade bhai, we were scared. We don't know what he did to make her so angry."

"Don't worry about that, I will take care," the Begum said, "Now go get ready. We will have lunch in half an hour." They all hugged her one by one and left in a lot better state of mind than they were in when they came in.

Rameela knew there was more to it than met the eye, but didn't know what. She had no intention of asking the Begum yet. So she too left the room quietly leaving the Begum to her thoughts.

Begum had other things to do than sit and think now. She knew that the situation was very explosive and there were forces at play, though she could not comprehend what they were. She knew one thing, though. She was powerless against them.

Shamim had aged and was only a shadow of what he was in his hey days. He was still a very powerful man against whom only a very few would dare to take chances. She was now convinced that the girl was possessed. Otherwise she could not have hurled Shamim like that. The very thought made her sick. So she walked determinedly to Shamim's quarters. She found him lying on the bed, pale and shaken. This only worsened her fears. She could not afford to lose him. Without Shamim, her gang of goons would be a useless pack of wolves, not the normal menacing Dobermans.

When he saw her, he sat up with some difficulty and said, "I have to deliver today or they will come after me."

"It was a huge mistake, Shamim bhai," she said, "Didn't I tell you, you were playing with fire? Now let us see what can be done. I don't want anything to happen to my girls."

As Rao reached home for lunch, Sanjay Saxena who was waiting at the gate informed him of the call from the Dehri police requesting him to contact them immediately. Rao rushed in and returned the call. The police had found a Toyota Qualis half submerged in the Sone Canal below the highway bridge with two dead occupants. The vehicle appeared to have strayed off the highway just before the bridge and fallen into the canal. The call ended with the understanding that they would keep him informed of further details after retrieving the vehicle and the bodies from the canal for which arrangements were already underway.

Even as he was completing that call, his mobile started buzzing. It was from Kharagpur crime branch. It somehow sounded ominous and made his heart sink in anticipation of some bad news. A body had been found on the steep slope of a deep gorge inside the dense jungle not far from the abandoned truck on the highway NH6. Nothing could be said yet about its identity except that it appeared to be that of a male. Homicide team was being mobilized to retrieve the body with assistance from the Forest Department. The task was not going to be easy as the place was very slippery after the 5 day storm. An inspector had already slipped and broken his ankle. Rao thanked them and called off after requesting them to keep him posted.

Death and bodies were nothing new to Rao to cause any discomfort or loss of appetite. But this was personal. Total lack of clues as to where his loving child was, and the suspense whether she was alive or dead was stealing his appetite and sleep. Yet he went through the motions ritualistically so as not to lose his balance. So he sat down to his meal.

Rana sat toying with his food as his mind was busy scheming and Bablu stood at a discreet distance watching his boss in silence. Pinto was aging but was still strong as an ox. He was not the type to fall ill and that too suddenly. But when a heavy man falls, he is bound to hurt himself. He turned to Bablu and said, "Let's give him two more days."Bablu replied, "We may not have the luxury. Rao may catch up soon."

Rana responded a bit pensively, "True. But there is nothing to lead him to Pinto as yet. That's precisely why we should give Pinto time. He will keep things quiet in his own interest. Meanwhile find out what's going on there. Something smells very fishy."

Bablu said, "In any case Pinto needs to be replaced sooner or later. The sooner, the better."

Rana grinned and said, "Come on. Who is it you have on your mind? Spill it out."

"Farooq," said Bablu. Rana knew it even before he asked him. Pinto was very discreet and highly trustworthy. He kept to his side of the deal and never probed. It acted as a firewall that shielded both sides. That's how they had got away so far and all investigations just failed. Some smart chaps like Rao could only suspect and were in the end left with nothing but only their suspicion. So, Pinto was very essential to maintain that. Bablu didn't understand these things much. Farooq on other hand was brash, boastful and loud mouthed, which was very bad for this business. It would be suicidal to bring him in. Like Pinto was not Pinto, Rana was not Rana. Very few people knew it. Bablu was not one of them.

"No, we can't bring him in on a live case of which he has no clue. He will have to be worked on and developed. So, forget it for now," said Rana. Though he said it quite matter of factly, there was an underlying chill that sent a clear and loud message to Bablu to dismiss such thoughts. He was not happy.

Farooq had his own ideas. He believed in moving fast. As the Begum left Shamim's room, she almost ran into Farooq. She took a couple of steps back in shock. With folded hands and a wicked grin he apologized for dropping in unannounced and expressed deep concern regarding 'bade bhai's' health. She glared at him and walked past briskly. Unmindful of her reaction, he went in and stood by Shamim's bedside. Shamim seldom reacted to anything and hardly revealed his mind. He just turned to his men and gestured to them to throw him out. When the men advanced menacingly, Farooq stepped back pretending to back off and said in a hurt voice, "This is not fair, bade bhai. I came here only to enquire about your health."

Patlu came in on the scene as if from nowhere. He was a martial arts buff and was self trained in the art. As Patlu made some menacing moves, a stiletto appeared in Farooq's hand as if by magic as he kept moving backward towards the door. As he reached the door, he saw Rameela and immediately grabbed her and put the knife to her throat. The Begum had sent her to shut out all entries to inner quarters to prevent Farooq from making further foray into the house.

Patlu was a great admirer of Rameela. She had a lithe body and carried it gracefully gliding like a swan. She did yoga, kept her body well groomed and took great care to maintain an angelic look. She was high class and looked every inch so. She catered only to the elite in society. He wanted to kill Farooq then and there. If looks could kill, Farooq would have been a dead man by now.

Farooq had not come here to retreat like a coward. He had come here to conquer and nothing was going to stop him. This dame on whom he had an eye all along fell into his hands like a moth in a spider's web. He was going to teach them who the boss here was from then on. So he dragged her in and when he saw a closed door, he asked her to open it. She kept still and said nothing. But Patlu moved in a flash and stood blocking the door and challenged Farooq.

Before Farooq could make any counter moves, Rameela, using her right hand, grabbed his right wrist holding the knife to her throat and pushed it away from her throat. At the same time, her left leg rose backward and hit Farooq's groin crushing the testicles between her heel and his pelvic bone. The man cried out hoarsely, dropped the knife and bent down in excruciating pain. As he did so, Rameela turned and raised her right knee to hit him in the jaw crushing his tongue between his teeth. He couldn't even cry now. She then dragged him to the outer door and flung him out on to the street below.

Patlu stood there gaping at her. He just couldn't believe his eyes. She had just done a Raquel Welch act. To Patlu, Bruce Lee was God but he worshipped Chuck Norris. Raquel was Goddess to him. As a teen ager madly in love with martial arts and cinema, he had seen her in a movie appearing in a black leather suit and bashing up the bad guys with a cat like grace. She had stood there with her long lean legs apart while confronted by four ugly strong men. She had then unzipped the top of her dress. As they stood gaping at her, her limbs flew left and right in swift motion flooring them all. She had floored Patlu too.

He could not believe that his Angel had done something even more fantastic. In a jiffy, she had reduced Farooq to pulp all the while maintaining her super cool. It had lasted just a few minutes.

Rameela saw and realized what she had done, unlike Shibani who had fainted and didn't know what she had done. Recovering herself quickly, she turned and walked away from the door as if nothing had happened. She went to the Begum's room and told her that Farooq had left and that they could have their meals in peace. After meals, when Begum returned to her quarters, Rameela told her calmly what had happened. She didn't have a clue as to how she could do it. She remembered distinctly what she had done and had experienced a fierce murderous rage while doing it.

The Begum was now very worried. First Shibani, now Rameela. The news should not get around. It was bad for business. While it would help keep the bad elements away, such news would drive customers away too. She detested the media the most. They would distort things and add on any nonsense their imaginative mind may invent for the sake of wider publicity and circulation.

She was not the only one who was worried.

Premnath was there sitting alone because of the afternoon lull in the business when he saw a hulk of a man being hurled out of the opposite house and that too by a girl, who was not even half his size. He had seen her before and wondered how she fit into the set up as she did not look one bit a whore. She somehow seemed not to belong here, yet there she was very much part of the house. The man appeared to be in great pain as he dragged himself away bent like a hunchback and spitting blood. The road was deserted and the next door workshop hadn't yet opened after lunch. He was probably the only witness. He didn't know who that ugly guy was but he was no pushover.

What worried Premnath were the strange things that had been happening in a row. First it was the man at his shop who had tripped and broken his nose, then the pimp who had helped him falling ill immediately and not being seen since and now this incident. Something was terribly wrong. He didn't know what. But, if such things continued and the media and the police landed, the place would be virtually shut down and business would be badly hit. It was the last thing he wanted on the heels of the almost week long drought in business due to the storm. That was what worried him most. He was also worried about the off and on strange feeling he had had of not being alone the last few days. He somehow felt that it had something to do with the bad lot who had dropped in on that stormy night asking for some pimp.

Shamim heard what had happened after they left his room. He immediately smelt trouble and desired to restore order. So he dismissed everyone including Patlu, his trusted one. With some difficulty he got off the bed, opened the locker and took a shot of Dianabol IV, an anabolic steroid. He took it very rarely because he didn't need it anyway but still kept it for any emergency. He still took some small dose of 25 mg twice a year. Now he took a 100 mg shot. He quickly restored the kit to its secret storage, closed the locker and went back to bed. Soon the drug took effect and he started feeling better.

Chapter 8

MYSTERY INTENSIFIES

Wednesday; May 27, 2009

Hyderabad

DCP Rao received information that the two dead men found in the SUV Toyota Qualis were identified as Kirpal and Jaggu, wanted criminals. The official who called wanted to know whether any ransom money was paid. Rao said, 'No' and enquired 'Why?' After a little while, the man at other end replied vaguely and said that the dead men were wanted criminals who specialized in kidnapping and extortion.

Kirpal and Jaggu were the followers of Daku (Dacoit) Man Singh of Chambal who surrendered in 2001. These men specialized in kidnapping women from villages. After the surrender of their boss, these men were locked up with other followers and released after six months. Once on their own, they formed a duo and engaged themselves in the only thing they knew well - kidnapping.

They would target a rich man who would be willing to pay a ransom to keep the matter under wraps and take his daughter or young wife. They took extra care not to hurt the victim and on being paid the ransom, they would release the victim and just vanish for some time to resurface later elsewhere. It lasted about 3 years before the law caught up with them. So in 2004, they were nabbed in Bhagalpur on a tip off. But no criminal charges could be pressed against them since the victims refused to identify them for fear of future safety especially given the Chambal background of the culprits.

The police still managed to keep them behind bars as under trials for four years. When the Bhagalpur Prison was being upgraded to Special category in 2008 to house terrorists and dangerous criminals, the inmates were shifted to another prison. It was then that they managed to escape from custody and were not traceable since.

They appeared to have driven under the influence of drugs, lost control and gone off the highway into the canal below. There was enough evidence at the site to indicate this theory.

Rao was informed that they would send him their description, tyre marks of their vehicle, post mortem reports and would keep the case open as long as he wanted and then would close the file and end the trial.

What they did not tell Rao was that they had found a bag full of cash worth a million rupees, to which there was no claimant. That was enough incentive to close the file and forget it.

Rao sensed as much. He received their description by fax. Neither matched the description of the man collected from the Toll Plazas on the highway. They must have been in the Qualis inside the container of the trailer truck abandoned on NH6.

The body from the forest was yet to be retrieved. He had to wait another day for that as was reported by the Kharagpur Police.

Bablu was driving at a steady pace of 60 kmph though the traffic on the highway was thin because his mind was busy. Soon after Rana had said 'No' to bringing in Farooq, he retired to his room and was planning to take things into his own hands when he received news from Farooq. On hearing details of the failure of his takeover bid, Bablu decided to pay a visit. Since Rana would never approve, he thought 'To hell with him' and set out to Kolkata quietly without informing Rana. What he did not know was that Rana knew about it and he too had left quietly by the evening but was headed in the opposite direction. Bablu did not realize that what he did suited Rana very well.

The only person who knew the real identity of Rana was the man at the wheel of the sedan. He could put any chameleon to shame. He specialized in impersonating targeted people to blend into any place or situation and any witness would swear to having seen the person impersonated. So he was a waiter, driver, servant, an executive, sales representative, a beggar but would pick on a real person and impersonate him. He was a great actor who could walk or talk like anyone and get away with it. He had no real identity, at least on record. Even during his espionage times, he was known only by different codes at different times. He left the field as quietly as he had entered it and left no clues behind that could return to haunt him. He had observed Rana from both outside and inside and blended into his affairs both legitimate and illegitimate. One day he would just melt away and Rana would never know. The man prided himself as the uncatchable 'shadow'.

Bablu was street smart. Though born in a fishing community, he was more interested in fishing in people's pockets and bags than in the Goan seas. At a very young age of 10, he was an expert in stealing from foreigners but one day he was caught red handed while stealing from a woman's bag, which had a hidden alarm in it. The moment he touched it, it raised such a huge racket that before he could even think of running, he was surrounded by people, a cop included. He was caught but he managed to give them the slip and run away. That was how he landed in Mumbai and from Charlie became Bablu. The huge crowds that traveled by the local trains gave him a field day. He was soon caught by local gangs operating there and thrown out. Wherever he went, he confronted the same problem. Everywhere there was a gang in operation and unless recruited by them, one couldn't survive. It was then he met the guy who took him as a marketing agent in his 'insurance' business. He provided commuters with insurance cover for ticketless travel. All they had to do was just pay 50% of their season ticket fare to the insurer. If the commuter was caught and fined, he just had to pay the fine and claim the same from the insurer. But if a guy developed cold feet and wanted to quit, he got a refund of the latest amount he had paid. The commuter had nothing to lose. As only about 5% of such commuters got caught, the insurer had a roaring business. Bablu enjoyed the 'job' he had landed – it seemed as good as the jobs most of his clients did.

Then came the day when a guy offered him a better job that would pay the kind of cash he had never seen in his life. Bablu was always bored with what he did because he thought he was made for bigger things. So when this offer came, he thought the day he was waiting for had arrived. He said 'YES' without any hesitation.

Mumbai Port, a premier port of the country has more assets outside the port than inside. It owns the most precious commodity in Mumbai - land - and plenty of it. The problem is most of it is mired in legal battles. One such battle seemed to be heading towards a favourable closure for the Port. There was a witness whose evidence would clinch it for the Port. The aggrieved party had tried to negotiate with the witness but failed, so they sent a party to scare him. The man was honest and bold. He told them to 'go and jump into the sea'.

As the date neared, the party got desperate and approached an underworld gang and they closed the deal. The gang had its own style of operation. The gang had eyes everywhere and they kept tabs on unknown commodities like Bablu.

After Bablu said, 'yes', he was kept under surveillance and was told what to do. All he had to do was shoot a guy from close quarters once in the chest and once in the head. He was to throw the gun on the guy and just walk away into the crowds. A car in the adjacent lane would pick him up and drop him off at the railway station where he would be met by a guy who would give him his ticket and a key to a suit case chained to his seat. He would also get a change of clothes. He could change into it in the car itself. He was not to come back to Mumbai for at least six months. He would find his fee in the suitcase.

He had agreed. It went off so smoothly that he could not believe that he had done it. Only on reaching Delhi and checking into a hotel had he checked his case. They had paid him two lakhs. He had spent the next two weeks enjoying his earnings visiting all the tourist spots.

While coming out of the Lotus temple, he had suddenly felt giddy and fallen. He vaguely remembered that a gentleman had come forward to help him up but beyond that everything had gone blank. When he woke up, he found himself in some hotel room in Kanpur. The surprising thing was that all his things including cash were there. No one had taken anything. Though quite puzzled, he took it in his stride and started exploring the city. In one of the restaurants, he met a gentleman and befriended him. After a couple of days, when the man asked him whether he would like to work for him, Bablu on some impulse said 'no'. The man left it at that and next day when they met again, he fished out a newspaper from his brief case and asked Bablu whether he knew the man in the picture. It was the picture of the man he had shot in Mumbai. Bablu then realized that he was dealing with some master crook and simply said that he was willing to work for him. That was how he had met Rana and joined him. He was pleasantly surprised when Rana started treating him like his right hand from the very first day. On the first job he was just to see and observe everything. He was amazed at the meticulous planning and discreet execution of the job. He was impressed and felt proud that he had at last graduated to the higher echelons of crime.

This was the second job and Bablu's first. He didn't want it to go wrong. So he had decided to take things into his own hands and show Rana what he was made of. The sudden blaring horn brought him to the present and he quickly swerved to his left. He had narrowly missed being knocked down. He slowed the vehicle and stopped it at the nearest way side hotel.

He sat there and decided what he would do on reaching Kolkata.

Rao and his team were engaged in their stock taking meeting.

The waiter in the restaurant who had attended to the table on the 24th swore that he had taken ill the previous evening and was laid up in bed the whole of next day. His family and neighbors confirmed the same. Even the doctor confirmed having treated him and was certain that he could not have attended duty that day. But the others at the restaurant also swore that he had very much worked there on that day and had attended to that table. So someone had very convincingly taken his place and played the part.

The vehicles used were all traced and they led them nowhere. The owners and the drivers were in the clear. The driver of the abandoned truck whose description was now available was yet to be traced but the body yet to be retrieved from the gorge not far from the abandoned truck could very well be that of the driver.

The possible suspects who carried out the kidnapping were also found but dead.

"That leaves us with nothing to go forward with and no clues as to the whereabouts of the victims," said the ACP summing up.

Everyone sat in silence as no one had any bright idea to suggest and a painful gloom set in.

DCP Rao broke the silence and said, "Yes. We have found the vehicles and the men who carried out the kidnapping, though dead. Their bodies were found very conveniently in the state in which they were wanted. But we have not found the victims or their bodies. What does that mean? They are still alive and are in the custody of the people who master minded the operations. The men who did it are known criminals who did it for a living and for ransom money. But, in this case they didn't make any demands because the money was paid by the people who hired them for the job. Apparently, the boy and the girl have not been taken for any ransom money but for sale either in the domestic market or in the international markets.

If the sale is to be made in the international markets, they would be heading towards the border.

Now, the question is which border. The truck used for the job was abandoned in West Bengal in a jungle on the state border. They may have headed from there towards Kolkata to the east for smuggling them across to Dhaka or to the west to the Pakistan border in Rajasthan or Punjab.

There is nothing to be done here. We should split into two teams and immediately fly to Kolkata and Delhi. We have already lost a lot of time. I have a hunch that something is going to happen tonight. So let's be there when it happens."

Chapter 9

HIGHTENED PREMONITION

Wednesday; May 27, 2009

Kolkata

Premnath too felt that something terrible was going to happen that night. He was having from the evening a growing premonition of some impending grave event. Business was brisk and everything looked bright and encouraging except for his uneasiness. So he was very alert and almost on edge.

Across the road, there was tension in the house as Shamim who had miraculously recovered to the delight of the inmates had later just disappeared. They searched for him everywhere, in vain. Patlu kept reassuring everyone that he would return and tried his best to keep things in control. The steady flow of customers kept the girls and the Begum busy.

Rameela had a busy schedule. But first she would visit her home, her foster home. Subir Das, a renowned Psychiatrist and his wife Protima Das had adopted her as their foster daughter. They did not have any children and shared everything in life and lived a very happy life until she passed away about 5 years ago. He always discussed all his patients with his wife, spoke about them, analyzed their character, their problems and even the remedies he had suggested. Rameela was no exception. They had discussed her problem too.

Rameela was born in a large Muslim family and was the eldest girl. As was customary in their family, they gave her away in marriage when she was still 16. The boy was the only son of rich parents and was spoilt beyond repair. He was a school dropout who roamed with scoundrels and had turned out to be a bad lot. His parents were advised that he would turn a new leaf if he was married. It was in that hope they had solemnized his marriage with Rameela, a beautiful girl with a good family background.

Their hopes proved to be wrong. He had scant respect for women and thought that their only purpose was to gratify the male desire for sex. So when he got a wife, he thought he had the license to use her as he pleased. To him going to the brothel was like going to the Bank. They had their working hours and rules and you had to follow them; but a wife was different. She was like an ATM. He said this to Rameela when she refused to consent during the day. He had no shame. So he would even shout and call her loudly using filthy language unmindful of the presence of his parents. They felt very embarrassed and regretted having got him married. But they could do nothing except go away to their village. This made things worse for Rameela. He made her life miserable.

When she discussed this with her mother, she was told that it would not last forever, these things are common between newlyweds and that she should learn to adjust. Other women she turned to said that she should make the most of it when it lasted because sooner or later the men would lose out their steam and leave you starved for more. One of them even said most men were incapable of satisfying their women, driving them to look for greener pastures or suffer for the rest of their lives. No one really understood her agony and her tortured emotions. The man wanted her even during her periods and forced himself on her. In short whenever he had an erection, he had to stick it into her no matter what time of the day or night or whether she was well or ill.

Rameela had actually taken up a job soon after their marriage to escape from his advances during the day. While some colleagues would tease her not knowing her sufferings, some in whom she had confided and sought advice from, understood her miseries and sympathized with her. Some of them would tell their own tales, which made her feel that she was not alone and maybe all women suffered at the hands of their husbands in some way or the other.

In the three years of their marriage she had two miscarriages because of his sexual adventures even during her pregnancy. She had come home after the second miscarriage after going through the trauma of dilation and curettage (D&C) feeling week in body and numb in mind. But what awaited her shattered her. Soon after her return he dragged her to the bed and forced himself upon her without a care for her cries of protest and pain. He told her that it was good that she had got the mess cleaned up. He compared it to a clean slate to write upon. This left her totally traumatized. She thought she would go mad. That was the time she visited Subir Das referred to by one of her colleagues.

After hearing all her woes, he had told her that her husband suffered from a condition called Algolagnia, a form of sexual perversion characterized by sadism and masochism. Such persons would derive pleasure from not only inflicting pain but also in experiencing it. If you resisted, they would take it as a challenge and turn more sadistic and violent. Total submission could be a remedy as they would lose interest and may look for somebody else to pick on. He had told her to try it but had also warned that it may not work as the man seemed to have gone overboard and become more of a maniac.

The next day she tried. It seemed to work. But soon he turned violent and hurled abuses at her calling her a bitch a few hundred times in the process. That set her thinking. She thought a bitch was far better off than any woman or wife. Even during the peak of a heat and while being chased by a dozen hungry dogs, she had the liberty to make a choice. She could choose one or more of them and also when and where. The dogs had no say in the matter. So why not become one, she thought and thanked him for planting the idea in her mind. The very thought made her feel liberated. So she left home never to return. She had heard from one of her colleagues about Sonagachi and the Begum who owned a high profile 'house'.

So when she met the Begum, she came directly to the subject and requested her to take her into her house. Despite all the abuses she had suffered at the hands of her husband, Rameela carried herself with dignity and self esteem. Her class came through. The Begum who was a good judge of people did not hesitate to take her in. So Rameela became a high class 'bitch' who showed men that she lived life on her terms and made her own sexual choices. She vowed never to allow another man to dictate her life or sexual choices. Her husband was arrested two days later while misbehaving with a woman in public and was locked up in an asylum when he turned violent and dangerous while in police custody.

Immediately thereafter she visited Subir uncle and Protima aunty and informed them of her liberation and the life she had chosen to live. They loved her like their child and appreciated the bold decision she had taken. So she visited them once a month and spent a few hours with them during which time she would listen to Subir uncle talk of Sigmund Freud and his theories, his works, his association with Carl Jung, how they differed in their theories. Sometimes he would talk of Jiddu Krishnamurthy and his philosophy. She liked the idea of living life directly moment by moment in the present and not through ideas, theories and words or in the past or future. She would narrate her experiences with men and he would give psychological interpretation of their behavior which both Protima and Rameela would enjoy. She would then leave after dinner. She continued to visit him even after aunty passed away.

Subir Das was 65 years old now and looked forward to her visits as it filled the void that had set in after Protima's death. The servants too welcomed her and loved her. It was difficult not to. She was such a nice girl who never treated them like servants. She left them feeling good about themselves and gave them a sense of self respect.

So she reached her home by around 6.30 p.m. Subir was delighted to see her and so were the servants whom she individually greeted and enquired about. During their usual talk, she told him of the incident involving Farooq and what she had done to him.

After hearing her and asking a few questions, he told her that it was the pent up anger she had been suppressing all these years which had erupted into violent action when she was in a life or death situation with a knife at her throat. When she asked why she did not feel any remorse or repentance for her action, he said it was possibly because the man represented all that she loathed in men. She still did not understand where she got such strength from. He smiled and said that the pituitary gland was a wonderful part of the human anatomy and what it could do defied all logic. In life threatening situations or when a person is in a state of extreme anxiety, a frail woman could easily overturn a speeding vehicle if that was perceived to be the object of threat. He then told her to forget it and not to worry about it. The bugger got what he deserved. What he said made perfect sense but somehow she was not convinced that it was as simple as all that. She felt that there was something more to the incident which was beyond their comprehension.

Around 9.00 pm she took leave of him promising to drop in twice a month instead of once, as he now wished. She had four calls to make before returning to the house.

It was around the same time Rao left for Kolkata and Rao's deputy Krishna Kumar for Delhi.

Rameela visited two star hotels where she had appointments with first an outstation businessman and then a foreign delegate to a local conference. She finished the second call by midnight and headed to a private guest house to spend some peaceful time with a respectable rich gentleman of Mumbai.

Chapter 10

THE FIND

Thursday; May 28, 2009

Kolkata

The man Rameela was visiting was a tycoon who was into everything from steel and cement to computers and software. He traveled extensively working without a break. He had no family life as such because his wife had deserted him for a Hollywood film star and his only daughter had chosen to live with an international soccer player in South America. So when he got tired of work, he would retire to his Kolkata guest house after spending four days at Shantiniketan.

Though he was all the time surrounded by many women who worked for him in various capacities across the globe, he desired the company of a Bengali girl who would appreciate music, particularly ghazals. After a lot of discreet enquiries and background checks, he had picked on Rameela and had taken an instant liking for the girl. She had class, intelligence, excellent taste and above all exceptional character. She never wished to know him more than he wished to reveal. She understood that he had not sought her for any sexual gratification but only for companionship. Her charming presence and her understanding of his emotional needs made her an inseparable part of his Kolkata visits over time.

They would recline on the bed next to each other and watch on the huge screen facing the bed classics such as Ben-Hur, Mughal-e-Azam, Casablanca, Taj Mahal, Pyasa, Pakeeza, Umrao Jaan and so on. But there would always be some ghazals in the end played softly over the surround system that truly surrounded them. He liked them all from Begum Akhtar to Pinaz Masani and Mehdi Hasan to Talat Aziz. He would doze off in the lap of the haunting music and she would quietly leave. During all this there would be absolutely no contact between them physically. He just desired that someone share his love for music and she fulfilled that desire perfectly.

When she was headed to the guest house, Rao was heading towards the city after his detailed meeting with the security head at the international airport. Bablu too had entered the city and was on his way to visit Farooq.

Premnath's uneasiness was growing as the premonition grew denser by the hour.

Across the street, the Begum too was feeling tenser by the hour for some inexplicable reason. Shamim was nowhere to be seen. She wondered how he could have gone off without a word to her after so many years of team work in managing the house. He was the wall on which she had leaned on all these years. She felt at a loss as to how she would manage without him if a crisis arose. Who would she turn to? She wished Rameela had cancelled her calls tonight. But she had dismissed Begum's fears and said it was too important a day for her to skip. She could not let them down. Begum missed her comforting presence.

She wondered whether she should call the priest and immediately, she felt terribly chill and felt like screaming but controlled herself. There was something eerie going on in the house. She could not discuss this with anyone except Rameela. She looked at the clock. It was only midnight. Shewould take at least 3 to 4 hours to return.

Bablu could not believe his eyes. Farooq was under sedation but he could see the bad shape he was in. He was utterly baffled that a woman had done this to a guy like Farooq. He also felt a terrible rage and wanted to teach the whore a lesson. So, he made enquiries about the girl and learnt that she always went out on calls but not every day and returned before day break. Further enquiries revealed that she was out on calls today. So he decided to wait outside and catch her as she returned. He wanted to show her in full public view the consequences of messing with them and putting spokes in their affairs.

Rao had spoken to Bipin Barua, IPS, his counterpart who was also currently holding additional charge of North Kolkata Division. They had agreed to meet first thing in the morning and Rao had decided to put up at Hotel White House near M.G Road.

All the officers in charge of Police stations falling under his Division were informed by Barua of Rao's visit and were requested to be available for an early morning meeting the next day. Pritish Mondal, the officer in charge (OIC) of Jorabagan Police Station, one of the stations under Barua's jurisdiction had retired early that day and had informed his deputy Keshab, Additional OIC to alert him in case of any emergency. The Additional OIC lived close to the station and had left the station to be manned by a sub inspector and a couple of constables.

It was 2.30 in the morning when Bablu reached Premnath's shop and sat down on the bench. Premnath became alert immediately as he felt that the worst he feared had landed.

Bablu ordered a cup of tea and biscuits and when Premnath handed them over, he asked him mockingly whether all was well. Premnath decided to keep mum.

"Do you remember? We have met earlier," said Bablu, trying to draw Premnath into conversation. But Premnath refrained from responding though he felt like telling him that scum like him were not worth remembering.

Just then another customer came and sat down and ordered tea. Bablu got into a conversation with him about the place and weather before asking him about the house across the street. The man replied that the dames there were not in his class. He thought they fleeced stupid fools who were under the illusion that they were high class. He asked Bablu, "You tell me what can be special about any woman when it comes to sex? Aren't they all the same? I remember dada muni's (Ashok Kumar) dialogue in one of the Hindi movies. He says all women are beautiful in the dark."Saying so, he laughed aloud. Bablu agreed and laughed with him. He said no whore was worth more than the mat they lie on. The conversation went on in this strain with the new comer quoting dialogues from several Hindi and Bengali movies. Bablu was amused to see that Premnath didn't like any of it. So he kept up the conversation just to irritate Premnath.

But it didn't last much longer as the man saw the pimp he was waiting for and rushed to get on with his business. Bablu sat on and told Premnath that the person he was waiting for was yet to come. Premnath told him to take a walk and come back later. This was no parking lot. Bablu stared at him for a while. As Premnath returned his stare without a flinch, he got up reluctantly and walked slowly away after paying him for the tea and biscuits.

Premnath knew that he would return.

Keshto was a driver attached to a travel agency which provided drivers to private car owners and companies on daily basis and sometimes on hourly basis. At times the owner of the agency obliged Government officials and provided drivers for free so that he could take favours from them in return. When it came to police officials he bent over backwards to offer them a free driver even for a whole day. The officials invariably treated them like servants. So Keshto hated to drive for them. But with market running dull and business hard to come by, there was no choice.

He had dropped OIC Jorabagan Mondal's guests at the airport and was returning empty. If it had been any private owner's car, he would have made some money by picking up a passenger. He knew that with police officials one could never take such risks. So sulking at the unfortunate circumstance, he drove in silence at a steady pace of 40 kmph.

At 3.30 am Rameela left the guest house quietly and headed back to the house. She had earned in one night nearly three times more than what a highly qualified and reputed senior finance professional would earn in a day. She had learnt that among professionals, only high profile lawyers earned more.

Bablu had returned within 15 minutes much to Premnath's dislike and anchored himself on the bench. As he kept ordering something or the other, Premnath could not ask him to leave. Moreover, Premnath was now convinced that the terrible thing he feared was going to happen sooner or later and that this scum would have something to do with it if not everything. So he let it ride. He was mentally prepared for whatever was to come and wanted to see it to the end.

As the car bearing Rameela drove into the lane, Bablu got up in anticipation. The car stopped in front of the house and

Rameela got out. Bablu had guessed right and was there in a flash. As soon as she closed the door and the car moved away Bablu grabbed Rameela, turned her around and gripped her throat. There were immediate squeals and screams that brought the Begum and some of her girls to the door.

Bablu heard a gruff voice say, "Let her go." He did not care and continued to squeeze Rameela's throat harder leaving her gasping for breath. This time Bablu felt a hand on his back and the words, "I said let her go" repeated. He said, "Go to hell." No sooner he said that than he felt he was hit on the head by a hammer. He immediately let go of the girl and swerved to find Premnath towering over him.

Rameela gasped for breath and coughed. Her throat and chest pained. Her eyes which had bulged returned to normalcy. Her vision was blurred by tears that had swelled from the dry cough. But she could see that the tea shop owner had come to her rescue and was now facing the scoundrel.

Bablu immediately took out a knife and flashed it at Premnath who hadn't expected that. So he stepped back. Encouraged by his retreat, Bablu flashed his knife at Premnath a few times and missed. Finding an opening, Premnath hit Bablu squarely on the jaw that sent him staggering back. Premnath quickly grabbed Bablu's hand holding the knife and squeezed it so hard that he cried out in pain and dropped the knife. Premnath then showered a series of blows that took the wind out of Bablu who was no match for Premnath. He kept hitting him relentlessly until the fellow fell flat on the road.

Premnath stepped back and so did the onlookers on either side of the road. The road was clear except for Bablu who slowly got up and started advancing towards Premnath with the knife he had picked up from the road. Keshto swung into the lane and on seeing the scene that confronted him, he applied the brake. To his dismay, the break didn't work. He hoped and prayed that the man would clear the road. Suddenly as if someone had grabbed him by the collar from behind and turned him left, the man was now facing the car and as Keshto desperately tried to apply the brake, the man advanced as if shoved from behind and staggered right into the car. Premnath, Rameela and others stood gaping as the car hit Bablu and threw him down, ran over him and stopped. Keshto found that the brake had suddenly worked after hitting and running over the man.

The whole thing happened in a flash. Keshto got out of the car and started blabbering that he had tried to stop but the break hadn't worked. He kept repeating that. Premnath calmed him down and wanted him to inform the owner first. When he learnt that the owner of the car was the OIC of a police station, he thanked the heavens because they would try to cover up the matter and not allow it to blow up. But then he could not rule out the possibility that they would frame him for the man's death. So the worst he had feared had happened.

Keshto calmed down and informed the OIC of what had happened. He was told to stay there and do nothing until the police from his station arrived.

As Premnath stood there another unexpected thing happened. Rameela came running to him, kissed him on the cheek and said, "Thank you bhaiya," and ran back to the house. She stood there at the door wondering why she had not felt the same rage she had felt when Farooq had attacked her. She thought of Subir uncle's theory that at that time she had pent up anger which had exploded in a violent action. She thought that maybe the anger had been spent and that was the reason why she had not been able to fight back the attacker. She wondered who this man was. She had never seen him before. In fact, that was what most people gathered there were talking about except Premnath.

But, no one left the scene until the S.I and the constables arrived. As they were taking stock of the situation and taking photographs, the Ambulance the Police had notified also arrived.

The Ambulance carrying the body left for the Government mortuary and the Police jeep left for the station with Premnath, Rameela and Keshto followed by the OIC's car driven by one of the constables.

The journey to the station, though short, seemed long as no one said a word. Each of them was assessing the situation from his (her) own angle.

At the station, Keshab, the Addl OIC was waiting. As soon as the party arrived, he asked Premnath, Rameela and Keshto to sit on the bench. Leaving the constable in attendance, Keshab went into the inner room with the S.I for a quick appraisal of the case. They waited for Mondal, the OIC. It was nearly 5.30 when the OIC arrived. They all stood up and Keshto started to say something but was stopped by the OIC. He went into his room and after a brief conference with his deputy and the S.I who had visited the scene, he called Keshto.

Mondal heard Keshto's version of what had happened. He was not convinced. He asked the S.I to take him into the other room and record his statement.

Premnath was the next to be called. Premnath, who always believed in speaking the truth, told them everything from the time the victim first showed up on the stormy night at his shop to the time he was knocked down by the car. Mondal felt that the man spoke the truth but he was not ready to buy the supernatural or para normal stuff because he didn't believe in them. He thought it was all humbug.

As the S.I took Premnath's statement and Rameela was called in, the constable was dispatched to the scene to bring two independent eye witnesses.

Rameela told them that she had never seen the man before and she did not know why he had attacked her. She also told them about Farooq and what she had done to him and that the attack could be related to that incident. She carefully avoided any reference to the bashing Shamim bhai got from Shibani. As to the actual cause of the man's death, what she said almost matched with what the other two had said word to word.

Mondal felt very uncomfortable with this invisible stuff which had grabbed and shoved the man before the approaching car and Keshto's word that the brake had not functioned only during the short time before he hit and ran over the man. He told Keshab to call the mechanic and have the vehicle checked thoroughly, particularly the brake.

The constable returned with two witnesses, a pimp and a middle aged woman. Each of them narrated the incident almost identically and said the same thing about the cause of death – the invisible hand. He thought the whole thing was crazy. Man murdered by a ghost? But what bothered him was that every witness said it with such conviction that it could not be dismissed entirely. He had to get to the bottom of it without wasting any more time. He decided to pay a visit to the place.

Leaving Keshto behind with the S.I, Mondal left for the place accompanied by Keshab and the constable, Premnath and Rameela included.

On arrival, Mondal and Keshab surveyed the scene of the incident and called a few people and asked them what they had seen. While a couple of them said they had not seen but only heard what had happened, the rest corroborated the statements of the other witnesses. The matter was getting on Mondal's nerves by now. So he turned and asked Rameela to show them her house. She led them into the house. Premnath too was asked to follow. In all the 50 years of his life he had never set foot into a brothel though he lived so close to it for the last 30 years. When he hesitated, Keshab shouted at him to move it.

As they entered the house, Mondal felt a strange chill. So did Keshab and Premnath. Rameela too felt it but rushed in to inform the Begum. But the Begum herself came out and greeted the police officials and asked them in. Mondal and Keshab went into the Begum's room and asked the others to wait outside.

As they sat next to each other, Rameela took Premnath's hand into hers. He wanted to shake her off but somehow he did not. It gave him a strange feeling he had never felt before. It was the same feeling he had felt when she had kissed him on the cheek and called him bhaiya. There was nothing new in it. He had been called bhaiya by so many people so many times. In fact most people who came to his shop called him that.

But no one had said it like she did. He realized she was talking to him and paid attention to her. She was saying how grateful she was to him for saving her life and was asking him to come and stay with them in the house instead of staying all alone in that small shop. He could not say anything but shook his head. Ignoring the same, she continued that even a brothel needed a man around the house. It was no exception. With Shamim bhai gone and none of the others being upto it, only he could fill the gap. At last he found his voice and said that he could not and added that one of them, indicating Shamim's men, could do it. She replied that they were good followers but not leaders, none of them. He laughed and asked her what made her think he was a leader. She said, "Anyone who can take care of himself and rise to rescue others without even being asked to is a natural leader."

She went on to say how they adored him and even called him a saint. He looked at her confusedly. She laughed and continued that it was easy for men to go to the Himalayas or some deep forest away from all human habitats and live like a saint. In fact they were not saints at all. It was people like him who lived in a place like Sonagachi surrounded by not just women but sex workers for 30 years and not even looked at one were real saints. While people just talk of celibacy, he had been devoutly practicing it for so long and amidst people like her.

As he fell silent and was in a confused state as to what was happening and why he was having the strange feeling in his chest, she pleaded with him to say just one word, 'yes' and nothing more. "I will take care of the rest," she said.

Though he wanted to cry hoarse a NO, he involuntarily nodded. That was enough to thrill Rameela. She said, "Thank you bhaiya, now there is no need for even that one word." She planted another kiss on his cheek and rose to rush in and tell the Begum. She stopped in her tracks as Mondal stood in her way, and asked her what the commotion was all about. She fell silent, dropped her head and said, "Sorry sir, nothing."

The long chat they had with the mistress had yielded nothing new. The strange chillness persisted. He decided to take a look around the place.

Going around the house, they reached a room which was closed and a girl stood outside it. Mondal said he wanted to see the room. The girl said, "It is my room. There is nothing to see. You can go." Mondal was struck by the strange behavior of the girl. He stood there and sized up the girl. She was small, maybe 20 years old, good looking, fair complexioned, black hair, big round eyes. When he looked into her eyes, he felt a strange feeling come over him. He felt cold and stiff. Then it passed off and he felt normal again.

He spoke to her gently and said, "Good. Why don't you show us your room? We won't take anything. We will just look around like we did the other rooms. That's all. There is nothing to worry."

As he spoke, he moved forward. He took just one step and then was unable to move any further. He could not comprehend what was stopping him. Keshab who was just behind said, "Sir, please wait. Let me talk to her."

Still feeling strange and uneasy, Mondal stepped back and let Keshab handle it. The Begum, Rameela, Premnath and others who were around held their breath and hoped the policemen didn't do anything stupid. Keshab took a few steps and stopped. He felt he was being pushed back and when he resisted, his chest started paining. He immediately stepped back and looked at his superior in dismay. Keshab was looking very ill. Mondal realized that there was something terrible wrong here. Maybe what his witnesses told him was true. But he was not giving up yet.

He signaled Keshab to leave. Rameela immediately came forward and helped Keshab retire into the adjoining room. She gestured to one of the girls to fetch something to drink.

Premnath was amazed by the presence of mind of this girl who had called him bhaiya and showered so much affection, something he had never known in all his life.

Mondal spoke to Shibani gently again and told her, "Ok. We will not disturb you now. We will come back when you feel up to it."

"No. Don't come back, if you care for your life. Nobody goes in there except me," said the girl. Mondal did not know what to make of it. Here was a girl as frail as a bird threatening to take the life of a seasoned policeman like him who was at least three times her size and five times her weight. He was not the type to give up that easily. So he said, "Sure, no one goes in there except you and me. No one else will go. Is that fine?"

"No, no, not you. No one goes in there except me and DCP Ram Manohar Rao sir. No one else," replied the girl. This took everyonc by surprise. Mondal's eyes almost popped out. He was baffled and lost all his composure for a minute. How in the world did this girl know of Rao sir? He understood that the matter was very serious and it was best left to the DCP to handle it.

He said, "Fine. I will inform Mr. Rao. So relax."

He backed off and gestured to everyone to leave.

Back in the Begum's room he told her and the others not to do anything until he returned with Mr. Rao. The Begum asked him who Mr. Rao was. He didn't care to tell her everything. So he just said, "He is the DCP crime branch in Hyderabad and is presently in Kolkata. I will return with him. Until then nobody does anything." Everyone nodded. Rameela asked him whether she was required to go back to the station with him. He thought 'clever girl' and smiled and said, "No need."

He turned to Premnath and said, "You too." Keshab had by now recovered and joined them. They left immediately leaving the constable on guard with the instructions that nobody may leave or enter the house until they returned.

They left the house but did not return to the station. They drove to the Hotel White House where Rao sir was staying. On the way they called their superior Barua sir and briefed him. He listened carefully and said he would join them at the hotel.

Back in the house, as Premnath prepared to leave, Rameela caught him by the wrist and said, "You cannot leave, sir. You are under house arrest. Didn't you hear the officer say, 'no one leaves the house or enters it until we come back'?" She bade him sit down and told the Begum that he had consented to move in to stay with them. He started protesting and said it was not true.

The Begum came forward, sat before him with hands folded in prayer and said, "Please, don't look down upon us. We are not bad people. The profession we are in may be shunned by society, the very same society which has pushed us into this life. This life is not so bad when you look at all the miseries that people suffer out there in the 'good' world. You are a man who has seen life and its various colours, I can say. I don't need to tell you. We want you to accept our invitation to come and stay with us. It will make us very happy. We assure you that you will not regret it. Like Rameela said we too need a man around the house and a good and kind man like you is the best we can ask for. But then we do not want you to feel any compulsion to accept our invitation. We leave it entirely to you. Whatever you decide, we will respect it."

Premnath sat in silence thinking about his life. From the time he had run away from the detestable woman called his mother, he had kept clear of women. The love and affection he knew was relegated to memories since the day he lost his father. During his formative years he had learnt from others the art of struggling with life. There was no place for any emotions in the life he had known so far. He had so far lived the life of a recluse who did not care for anyone nor did anyone care for him whether he was well or ill. Many times he had wondered what the purpose of his life was. But he could never understand and had dismissed such thoughts as foolish fancy, saying to himself 'everyone comes into the world alone and leaves it alone.' It was probably this day he was waiting for. May be this was his destiny. He had always accepted his life as God's will. So he thought he would leave it to God.

He did not know what it meant to have a brother or a sister. Such affections were alien to him. So when Rameela showered her affection, he was overwhelmed by it. When he thought back at the trail of events in his life, particularly the past few days, he thought maybe it was God's will that had landed him here in this situation. So if that was God's will, then that is what it would be.

Mondal and Keshab reached the Hotel almost at the same time as their boss Barua. Rao was waiting for them eagerly having been told by Barua that things seemed to be heading towards a closure.

As soon as they were in Rao's room, Mondal narrated the incidents at Sonagachi in the early hours leading to his visit to one of the upmarket houses and the strange happenings there.

Immediately they left for the Begum's house. As soon as Rao entered the house, the atmosphere in the house changed dramatically. Shibani came running to Rao, held his hands and said, "My God, you have come at last, uncle. I can now rest."

Then she slumped and fainted. The Begum rushed and took the girl in her arms and tried to wake her up.

Rao, meanwhile, advanced cautiously towards the closed door, knocked and turned the door knob. He opened the door slowly but as soon as he saw his darling daughter, he threw open the door and rushed in. Sapna, on seeing her father sprang from the bed and ran into his open arms.

He was overwhelmed with joy and cursed himself for not having thought of this possibility. If he had, he could have found her earlier.

She cried in joy uncontrollably. Rao mistook that and asked her anxiously whether anyone had harmed her. She shook her head and quickly regaining her composure told him that the girl Shibani had taken great care of her. She had ensured no one entered the room. She brought her food, gave her clothes to changeand assured her that no harm would come to her. Sapna did not know how she managed but she had kept her promise. In fact, Sapna had not seen any one in the past 4 days except Shibani.

She then enquired about Suresh Babu. Rao realized that she might not be aware that Suresh too was abducted. As he was wondering what to say, Shibani entered as if to save him from the dilemma. On seeing Shibani, she ran to her and holding her hand came back to her father's side and introduced her to her father. The girl said, "Namaste, sahib." There was no recognition otherwise. Rao could not believe that it was the same girl who had come running to him on arrival and called him uncle. Mondal and Keshab could see that she did not recognize them either. Another significant change they felt was that the house was no longer chill and unwelcome. It was quite warm.

Everyone was totally surprised to find the new girl. No one except the Begum and Shamim knew of her, other than Shibani.

The police took the Begum and Shibani into custody for questioning. Keshab took them to the station.

Mondal accompanied DCPs Barua and Rao and his daughter Sapna to the Divisional office. He recorded Sapna's statement. She remembered Suresh having fallen sick at the restaurant and their deciding to leave. As they came out of the side entrance as usual, she felt someone grab her. Before she could resist, she felt a pin prick on her neck and everything became hazy and then there was total darkness. When she started waking up from some deep sleep, she thought she heard a girl scream. It was very faint, though. She thought she was being carried and so she tried to struggle. Then she felt drowsy and fell back into the darkness. When she woke up, she found herself on a bed and a girl stood watching her. The girl said, "Don't worry, no harm will come to you. I will see to it."

Sapna continued, "Then I must have passed out again. When I woke up, I found the girl again. The girl was very kind. She first asked me to wash up and change into some new clothes she had set by the bedside. By the time I returned from the washroom, she had some milk and snacks. She forced me to have some food first and then she told me that I was in Sonagachi, a red light area in Kolkata and that I had been brought there by a Shamim bhai, probably to be sold to some buyer. She then assured me that she would ensure that it doesn't happen. She then told me she was Shibani and then narrated her story and how she was given refuge by the Begum, the mistress of the house, whom she called her mother. She also said that the Begum was a good woman who did not force anyone into the trade."

Sapna had not seen anyone else until her father appeared this morning. The girl had kept her promise. Sapna did hear some commotion outside the door a few times but in the end it was always the girl Shibani who came in and locked the door.

She had no idea what had happened to Suresh Babu. When asked whether she knew that he too had been abducted along with her, she answered in the negative. She then started crying and demanded to know what had happened to her boy friend.

They told her that there was no news yet of where he had been taken and that the police were investigating. They assured her that they would find her friend and also the abductors.

Immediately after finding Sapna, Rao had informed his wife and assured her that their girl was safe and unharmed. Nandini took the first flight to Kolkata and was on her way.

On returning to the station, Mondal proceeded to interrogate Sardari Begum, the mistress of the brothel in the presence of her lawyer, a leading advocate who practiced in the High Court of Kolkata and the Supreme Court. She knew that Shamim was involved in some activity other than the one he was engaged in at her house, i.e., providing security to the inmates and warding off unwanted customers but she had no knowledge of what that activity was.

On the night of 25th May when he brought a girl and housed her in a room on her premises, she had protested. He said that she would stay there for a day or two and then leave. On being asked who she was, he had told her that it was none of her business and had become quite intimidatory. She had no knowledge of who the girl was or any other details about her. The girl remained confined to the room until this morning. As for the whereabouts of Shamim, she had no clue. He had suddenly disappeared yesterday without a word to anyone.

She further told them that all his things were still there in his room and that no one had touched anything. The police were at liberty to search his room. On being asked what the man looked like, she gave them a fair description of Shamim.

Shibani too gave a statement in the presence of the same lawyer and corroborated the Begum's story and added that she had protested and screamed at Shamim for playing with the life of an innocent girl and that she would not permit it. She promised the girl that she would see to it that no harm came to her and she had kept her promise. On being questioned as to how she knew DCP Rao Sir, she said the girl had told her who she was.

Mondal informed the lawyer that the police would register a case against the Begum under IPC Sec. 343 for wrongful confinement of a person for three days or more and under IPC 368 for wrongfully confining or keeping a kidnapped or abducted person. No charges were leveled against Shibani. The lawyer used his influence to prevail upon Mondal to release the Begum on personal undertaking from her lawyer. By noon, the lawyer had produced a Court order to the effect too.

Meanwhile, Nandini reached Barua's residence where Sapna was waiting for her. She was much relieved and delighted to see her daughter alive and unharmed. Sapna changed into her own clothes her mother had brought along. After lunch, they proceeded to meet the Begum and the girl Shibani. At the house, they found Mondal and his men searching one of the rooms. On enquiry, they were informed that the police were searching Shamim's room for evidence and clues to the abduction.

Much to his relief and as expected by him, Rao had received information that the body found in the gorge was that of the driver of the truck and it matched the description the police had obtained from toll plazas the previous day. He was a known offender and a car thief on police records.

The description of the man who had died in the morning at Sonagachi was sent to all major metros and state capitals. By noon, news arrived that it matched the description of the man who was wanted in Mumbai for murder.

Rao's family thanked the Begum and Shibani profusely for saving and protecting their daughter and promised to extend any assistance they may require. They were also requested to immediately alert Mr. Mondal in case they were contacted by Shamim or if they got any clue regarding his whereabouts. They then called at the Jorabagan police station and took leave of Mondal and his team thanking them profusely for all the assistance in finding their daughter and for their quick and efficient handling of the events of the morning. Finally taking leave of the Baruas, they left for Hyderabad.

Mondal's search of Shamim's room did not yield any positive clues as to the identity of the man or his dealings. They could not get even a single photograph or document to establish his ID. All they had was the description the Begum had given. It was fine tuned after talking to the members of the house.

Jorabagan P.S. flashed the description of Shamim to all the police HQs with the request to circulate it to all the stations under them. Several charges were filed against him.

EPILOGUE

When Shamim had called to inform Rana of the incident involving Farooq, he was told that he could expect Bablu there soon and was advised to lie low. Shamim had simply replied he knew what to do and called off. He realized that the mission had failed this time. The police were bound to come very soon. There was no way he could get the girl out before that. The best option was to abandon the mission. So, he had just disappeared quietly from Sonagachi leaving no clue behind that could establish his identity

Rana's previous endeavors in human trafficking were quite successful but this one seemed to have gone wrong. So he was advised by the shadow to get back to his legitimate front and stay put for some time. Rana always listened to reason and always believed in taking the emergency exit door in case of trouble. So, he had returned to Bhatinda from his 'business trip' as his real self Rudra Pratap Randhawa.

Three months later, a body was found in Varanasi that matched the description of Shamim. But the locals said he was a known wandering hermit who was seen off and on in Varanasi for more than a decade but no one knew him personally enough to throw any light on his identity.

The Begum was let off with a nominal fine as the charges against her could not be proved with conviction or sustainable evidence.

Suresh Babu was never found. Kirpal and Jaggu had tossed his body into the river on reaching Kolkata. The river which was in full spate and flowing furiously had consumed him instantly.

With Sapna safely delivered to her parents, his soul rested in peace.

JEEVA

Chapter 1

THE WILL

"Hello Mr. Arokiaswamy, how are you," enquired the doctor as he entered the room. Arokiaswamy, who was lying on his bed sat up with some effort and said, "You should be the one to tell me how I am doing, Dr. Shankar, isn't it?" Before the doctor could reply, he continued, "Because you are the one who is keeping me alive."

The doctor laughed and said, "It is HE who keeps us all alive. Wc doctors only assist people lead a healthy life and live longer. As for you, Sir, there is nothing wrong with you. It is just the age and the hard life you have lived that have caught up with you. You will live to be 100 and who knows we may go ahead of you."

"Now tell me why you summoned me, Sir" asked Dr. Shankar. Arokiaswamy nodded his head in silence and was about to say something when there was a knock on the door. Devanesan, the faithful servant who was standing behind the bed went and opened the door. Advocate Akbar Ali walked in and greeted the two of them. He took his seat on the chair next to the bed and said, "So, how do you do, doctor?" "Very well," replied the doctor and enquired the same of the lawyer.

Arokiaswamy asked Devanesan to get some snacks and tea for the guests. When Devanesan proceeded to execute the order closing the door behind him, Arokiaswamy told the doctor that he had asked the lawyer to draft his will and that he wanted him to be a witness to the same. That is why he had requested him to come this evening.

The doctor said, "I just told you that you may live to be 100." Arokiaswamy replied, "You also said something like one can never say who will go ahead of whom."

The lawyer joined the conversation and said, "It is always better to leave a will behind so that the ones you leave behind may not run from pillar to post to get what is due to them. If a person dies intestate, he leaves a whole lot of problems to his heirs and invariably they have to fight long legal battles or go through hell with the revenue authorities."

The doctor said jokingly, "Isn't that good for your business? So, why do you suggest a will?"

The lawyer said a bit mockingly, "It is like the Master Health Checkup you doctors recommend even to young people. Prevention is better than Cure." They all laughed, the doctor, a little sheepishly.

Devanesan knocked and entered the room pushing the tea trolley. Arokiaswamy asked him to lock the door and wait outside.

They continued their chatter and small talk through the tea session and fell silent as Devanesan took the trolley aside. Ali took out the will and gave it to Arokiaswamy, who gave it to Dr. Shankar to read it.

On reading it through, he silently handed it back to Arokiaswamy, who went through the document and asked, "Well, shall I go ahead and sign it?" Ali said, "Yes" but the doctor said a little hesitantly, "Is that really what you want to do with all your property and money?"

Arokiaswamy asked in a serious tone, “Do you doubt my sanity, Dr. Shankar?”

The doctor hastened to say, “No, no, that is not what I meant. I just wanted to be sure. It is the money and property you have worked hard for and earned. So, you are free to do what you will with it. If the same had been inherited, you wouldn’t have had the freedom to do as you please. Am I not right, Mr. Ali?”

“You are quite right. Since everything that is there is the fruit of his labour, he is at liberty to do with it as he pleases,” replied Ali.

“Can I sign now, doctor?” asked Arokiaswamy. “Please,” replied Dr. Shankar.

So the ‘Will’ was signed, witnessed, enclosed in an envelope and sealed by Akbar Ali and tucked away in his leather bag. After a little while, the visitors took leave of Arokiaswamy and he lay back on the bed, a little tired but a whole lot relieved at having made the ‘Will’.

He hit the ‘Replay’ button inside his head and went back in time.

Hailing from a rural background he had arrived in the big city Coimbatore and done all sorts of menial jobs before settling as a peon in a large factory. Though the job did not pay very well, it provided him the opportunity to meet a variety of people that included both suppliers and customers. It also provided him the opportunity to pocket small sums of money from the numerous errands.

He started lending that money to the factory workers on very handsome interest. Soon he started looking more respectable than he was. That helped him make friends with successful people with ideas. He shamelessly borrowed from them and adapted them into his dealings. From a petty money lender, he became a chit fund operator. Over time it grew into a chit fund company. He was once told that only money makes money. He had not understood it then. But he did now. He had also learnt that money was a good servant but a bad master. So he never allowed money to rule him.

He was rolling in money, though not his own. Soon he met a nurse by name Mary, fell in love with her and married her. As a single child, Mary inherited money and property from her parents. She sold the property and invested the money in his business. They were shrewd enough not to give up their humble jobs which kept them rooted to the ground. They lived a happy life. Their only regret was that they did not have any children. He did not mind it but Mary wanted a child badly. So she wanted to adopt a poor boy, a distant relative of hers. Arokiaswamy was not happy about it, but he could not say no to Mary, whom he loved dearly.

So they adopted the boy named John. He turned out to be a scoundrel of the first order. It affected Mary very badly. Arokiaswamy tried all he could to correct the boy, but in vain. The guilt and pain took a toll on Mary and she fell ill. Arokiaswamy consulted a number of doctors but there was nothing any of them could do unless she stopped blaming herself. One day she passed away in sleep leaving Arokiaswamy with the brat. One lucky thing was that Arokiaswamy had not adopted John legally. They had just brought him up. Arokiaswamy knew that John would remain with him in the hope that he would inherit all his property and money. He was not proved wrong.

He was brought back to the present by Devanesan who knocked and entered with his supper. Arokiaswamy had stopped having meals at the table since a month as he wished to have his meals in peace.

Chapter 2

THE WAY

Adams & Angels was a twin beauty salon for men and women. No, it was not a unisex salon. They were two adjacent salons under one roof and one management and one sign board. While one catered to men exclusively, the other did so for women.

Both the men's and women's sections of the salon had wash rooms at the back. In addition to the usual facilities and doors that one would normally find in a wash room there was a separate unmarked door a little away which would normally go unnoticed. If by accident or out of curiosity, one were to open the door, he or she would find what looked like a not so clean backyard with dustbins, drains and the like. If one ventured out of the door and looked around, he or she would find a poorly lit stair case.

If one ventured up the stairs, he or she would end up in a posh reception with a highly polished desk, luxurious sofa set, a wall adorned with photos of deities duly garlanded and lamps and incense burning before them. What was conspicuously missing there was a name. But an accidental visitor would not notice that. The immediate reaction of such a visitor would be to turn back and retreat hastily feeling guilty of having explored someone's territory uninvited.

The receptionist hidden behind the desk would promptly see everything on his screen. If the visitor retreated, he would leave it at that after capturing them on his system. If the visitor ventured to find more, he would appear and enquire. Almost everyone would apologize and return. If someone did not, he would alert the management and they would take over.

If the visitor happened to be a known customer, he would come forward and greet. If it happened to be special guests, he would remain discreetly invisible.

So when a gentleman known to him as Jose sir and a lady known to him as Grace madam had arrived separately with a 10 minute gap, he had remained seated behind the desk.

The two of them had their own keys to Room No. 2A. The place provided total privacy to the couple for their secret rendezvous.

They were sitting on the bed with pillows propped to their backs. She said she was tired of meeting like this and if he didn't do something about it, she would stop coming to him.

He told her he had a fool proof plan this time and that he would succeed. Then such meetings won't be necessary, he promised.

She got up, dressed and left saying that he better stop talking and start doing. She took an auto rickshaw to a small street behind a large mall, paid the auto fare and entered the mall through a rear entrance. After a while, she came out of the main entrance and called for her chauffeur driven car.

Ten minutes later, the man too left the private lodge. He returned to the salon, got his hair styled and left through the main door. He walked a couple of blocks to where his motor bike was parked.

As Arokiaswamy finished his supper, he heard the car enter the compound. Devanesan made a hasty but discreet exit with the supper tray. Soon, Jessy knocked the door and entered his room. She came and sat on his bed and enquired about his health. He replied curtly that he was well. She kept up the one sided conversation telling him what she had seen at the mall, about the ever increasing price of everything from pins to perfumes. Eliciting no response, she asked him about her latest hair style and whether he liked it. He grunted a yes. After making a lot of fuss about how worried she was about his health and planting a kiss on his cheeks and forehead, she made him lie down and tucked him into the bed. She then dimmed the lights and before leaving said, "Good night, darling. Sleep well. Everything will be alright soon."

But he did not sleep. Though he hated her, he could not bring himself to shout at her or even be rude to her. So he just ignored her. When it came to her, he blamed himself for having been such a fool, an idiot of the first order.

It was 5 years to the day since he had met her. He had come out of the church on a Sunday and as he turned left onto the main road, something hit his car on the offside. So he stopped and went round to see a woman lying unconscious by the side of the car. With some help from other drivers who had stopped their vehicles, he got her into his vehicle and took her to a hospital. Once she regained consciousness and was pronounced fit to leave, he had offered to drop her wherever she wanted to go. She thanked him and said he could not because she had nowhere to go.

On being probed, she told him that she was living in an orphanage and when she learnt that the manager and the watchman were planning to sell her to some brothel, she had fled with whatever money she had. She really did not know where to go. As she did not wish to reveal more, he did not press. But taking pity on her, he offered to provide shelter under his roof until she could decide where to go.

That was how she had arrived at his place. She showed a lot of gratitude and took good care of him. Soon he fell for her. Sensing the same, she offered to leave not wanting to be a burden to him or spoil his name in society. He fell for that too and in a fit of fancy offered to marry her. She protested and said he had a son who was old enough to be her elder brother and that she did not want to be the cause of a rift between the father and the son. He had dismissed her reasoning saying neither was he a father nor was that ruffian his son. He had married her in haste. This had indeed led to a showdown between him and John but in the end as Arokiaswamy had nothing to lose and John everything to lose, the matter was settled and John was allowed to continue to live in the house but strictly on the terms Arokiaswamy laid down.

The marriage brought some cheer and joy to his life for sometime but very soon he realized the futility of the relationship, though she seemed to make every effort to adjust. John expressed his hatred towards Jessy in every possible way and she totally ignored him which only made him seem more furious. To avoid an open confrontation, they seemed to avoid each other. While he remained out of the house most of the time, she seemed happy to stay indoors confined to her room except for going out once a week.

Despite the apparent animosity between them, Arokiaswamy felt that something was fishy, though he could not place it. So, he had his faithful servant and the driver spy on them. They were very watchful and reported everything to him, which in fact revealed nothing to confirm his suspicion or otherwise. In any case, he despised both of them and felt that he would have been happier without them.

His thoughts were interrupted when Devanesan entered with the routine glass of milk that he took every night as advised by the doctor. While he drank the milk, Devanesan reported what he had observed. Devanesan then removed the empty glass and returned with a water jug and a glass. He wiped the jar and the glass with a clean white cloth and left them on the bedside table. He then retired.

A short while thereafter, the driver came and reported. After parking the vehicle, he had gone inside the mall and looked for her everywhere but could not find her. Yet, she had come out of the mall after nearly an hour and a half with some petty purchases. However, he could have missed spotting her if she had been inside one of the beauty parlours. Arokiaswamy was suspicious and almost certain that she had given him the slip and returned to the mall unnoticed after a while but there was nothing to prove his suspicion. So he thanked him and dismissed him. The driver left after receiving the customary Rs. 100/- for his services. Arokiaswamy did not rule out the possibility that the driver may have received a bigger tip from her to keep his mouth shut.

Just then the door opened with a bang and John entered the room. He came straight to the bed and touching Arokiaswamy's feet started apologizing for having let him down so far and started making promises of turning over a new leaf from then on. As usual he was drunk. Arokiaswamy managed to get his feet free from his grip and sat down and started shouting at him to get out of his sight. He then started coughing. Immediately John took the glass, poured some water from the jug and held the glass to his mouth. Arokiaswamy took a gulp and then pushed him away still coughing a bit. John apologized and said, "Okay, sorry. Please sleep well. I will see you tomorrow. Please don't be angry with me, I beg of you." He again tried to touch his feet but Arokiaswamy pulled them away. John apologized some more and left staggering out of the door. He came back, said sorry and shut the door with a bang.

Arokiaswamy was shaking with rage but tried to calm down. As he prepared to stretch himself, he found a small bottle. Without touching it he bent down to see what it was. On finding that it was a bottle of sleeping pills, he picked it up gingerly with a hand kerchief and laid it on the side table. He sat there looking at it for some time. So, John was planning to kill him. Probably he planned to make it look like natural death.

Now that he had made his will, Arokiaswamy decided that he would turn the tables on them and implicate them for his death. If he died of an overdose of sleeping pills, it would look like suicide. But if the bottle and the water glass had no finger prints of his, then suicide would be ruled out. Then the person whose finger prints are found on them would become a prime suspect for murder.

John had held the glass of water to his mouth when he coughed. So he had left his finger prints on the glass and the jar and also in all probability on the bottle of pills as well. He would be the prime suspect. He hoped that if the police probed enough, they could implicate her too as an accessory to the murder. He didn't care if they failed to as he himself was not sure of that. In any case, he decided to go ahead with his plans.

Having decided to take his own life at the cost of John and Jessy, he sat and prayed for a while and then silently spoke to his dead wife Mary. He asked her to forgive him for what he planned to do to John. He also apologized to her for having given a place in his life to the schemer Jessy and said that he had made amends for the same in his Will. He then told her that he would join her soon.

He then slowly emptied all the pills into the glass, which was almost full as he had taken only a gulp when John had held it to his mouth. He took care not to leave any prints of his own. He then closed the empty bottle and let it gently roll down under the bed. He let the pills dissolve and after one last prayer, he drank the contents and kept the glass back on the side table. Holding a kerchief to his mouth, he gently stretched himself on the bed.

Chapter 3

THE END

At 6.00 a.m the following morning, Devanesan knocked gently on the door and entered the room with the morning coffee for his master. He froze in his stride and dropped the tray, shocked at what he saw. He could not believe that his master was no more. Recovering quickly, he closed the door, locked it from the outside and called Dr. Shankar.

Though it was quite early, Dr. Shankar rushed immediately to Arokiaswamy's place after alerting Advocate Akbar Ali of the event. The lawyer too, an early riser, left immediately to join the doctor. Before doing so, he informed the Inspector of Police of the area of Mr. Arokiaswamy's death and voiced his concern of a possible foul play. He could not believe that only the previous day they had met and he was quite well then.

Jessy was also up and standing by the window of her room on the first floor when she saw Dr. Shankar's car entering the compound. She immediately dressed up and came down the stairs as the doctor entered the house. She greeted him and enquired what brought him so early in the day. He acknowledged her greeting with just a nod of his head and followed Devanesan to Arokiaswamy's room. She too followed them.

When Devanesan opened the door, the doctor proceeded to enter. But he stopped and stepped back. There was no doubt of his death. Jessy who too saw the dead man, gasped and started crying aloud. When she tried to rush to her husband, the doctor stopped her. She started screaming at the doctor and asked him to do whatever he could. By this time the lawyer arrived. After taking in the scene, he cautioned Jessy not to enter the room or touch anything, in her own interest. She turned on him and screamed at him to do something instead of talking rules.

He calmly replied that he had already initiated what was required to be done. They closed the door and waited in the drawing room. By about 7.00 a.m the Inspector of Police arrived with his assistants in tow. After taking a look at the room, he ordered everyone to remain in the house and not to enter the room. His assistants took up position blocking all entries and exits to the house.

The Inspector mobilized the forensic team and informed the Government hospital and requested them to send an ambulance to carry the body for a post mortem. Devanesan informed Rev. Fr. Francis of the demise of his master, Mr. Arokiaswamy. The father expressed his condolences and said he would make the required arrangements for the funeral. As they waited, the Inspector questioned and took statements from the servant Devanesan, the watchman, the gardener and the driver.

He then questioned Jessy and recorded her statement. She seemed to have recovered from the early shock and regained her normal composure. She had switched on her acting talents and presented the picture of a poor innocent widow. The Inspector then requested the doctor and lawyer for their statements and they obliged readily.

When he enquired if there was any one left, Devanesan informed him of John who was still asleep in his room on the ground floor. The Inspector chose to let him sleep for then. The forensic team arrived around 8.00 a.m and immediately plunged into work. By the time they were done, the ambulance was ready. Meanwhile, the doctor and lawyer took leave of the Inspector and ignored Jessy.

At about 10.00 a.m the Inspector knocked on John's room and closed it from inside. Except for John's wailings in the beginning and the Inspector's stern voice a couple of times, nothing was heard outside. After recording John's statement and warning him not to leave the house, the Inspector left.

Two days later, Arokiaswamy was laid to rest in the Church cemetery ceremoniously. The funeral was attended by a large number of people. Jessy played the perfect widow and gained the sympathy of many in the crowd. John was not present at the funeral as he had been taken into custody as the prime suspect. Amidst the proceedings, the gossip was on in full swing. Some even looked at Jessy with suspicion.

The police charged John with murder. All the evidence was against him. He protested and tried to blame Jessy for the murder. The police investigation did not reveal any clue to that effect and so they did not press any charges against her, though she too had a motive.

The lawyer, as the executor of the Will pronounced the details of the Will to John, ín the presence of the police, Jessy, Devanesan and others. Arokiaswamy had left all his money and the gold ornaments in the locker to the Church. The Church was at liberty to use them for any charitable purpose. The house and all its belongings were left to Devanesan for his selfless service. He was at liberty to sell the house or retain it for his own use or for letting out on rent. He was the master of the house. The automobiles including the motor cycle was to go to the factory that had laid the foundation for his life.

John and Jessy were left with nothing other than what they had already been given. They were to vacate the house immediately after the funeral.

So, John was in the jail and Jessy back on the street again.

She could not believe that John had done it. He was not capable, which she knew only too well. She suspected that the old man had done himself in and framed the scoundrel, as he called him.

Anyway, she was free from both of them. Good riddance, though she could have got a better deal. What the old man did not know was that she had stacked away a sizeable sum in her bank account held in her original name, Jeeva.

She told herself, "Don't worry Jeeva. There are enough stupid men with lots of money out there in the world. All you have to do is find the right guy, which is not a big deal anyway."

As she sat on her berth in the 2AC coach on the train bound for Chennai, she kept gauging all the men around. Beware rich stupid men; Jeeva is on the prowl again.

MY GOD IS NO MORE

Chapter 1

THE ACCIDENT

The beggars were busy calling out to the devotees visiting the temple for alms. The temple would close in half an hour. So the attendance was thin. Buchi Babu too was looking for a prospective donor who may throw a coin into the plastic plate in front of him, which he kept tapping to draw attention.

It was nearing one month since he was 'contracted' to beg in front of the temple. Every one of them had a location allotted. They were not at liberty to change the location without the approval of their contractor. He reflected back on how he came to be sitting here and begging for alms.

It was a hot Sunday morning when he decided to take to begging and chose a vacant spot between an old woman and a lame man on the left side of the entrance to a popular Siva temple in North Chennai. The road leading to the temple from a main road bent to the right and connected to another main road. With increasing traffic on the main road, this link road had become a busy thoroughfare. To the left of the entrance to the temple, there was a small lane which was unsurfaced and uneven besides being narrow and slushy. The lane led to an old abandoned building that served as the 'home' to these beggars.

As he sat down in the vacant slot, the others protested and said that he could not sit there leave alone beg. When he didn't pay any heed to their protests, they warned him that he will have to face the consequences. Still he ignored them and continued to sit there.

He had not eaten anything since the morning and also the whole of the previous day. He had been surviving on just water. He felt weak and tired. Without warning, he received akick in the back that sent him sprawling forward and he lay there on the road looking up. A man came forward and demanded to know what he was doing there. Instead of replying him, he said to the man to at least wear a loin cloth or let the lungi down. It took the man a little while to understand what the old man had said. He raised his leg to stamp on the man's chest and realized what he had said. So instead of stamping on him, he stepped back and let the lungi down. The other beggars who were silent until then laughed in chorus. He shouted at them to stop and ordered the old man to get up.

As Buchi Babu rose, the man grabbed him by the collar and dragged him along the narrow lane to the old building. He did not know how else to react to the audacity of the old man. What he liked about it was the man had demonstrated that though he was down, he was not out. The old man had character. He was willing to fight against odds without losing his sense of humour.

He introduced himself as Perumal and said that he had taken the place on lease and the beggars were on 'contract' with him. So there was no place for any unauthorized person to trespass on his territory. On learning that the old man had not eaten for two days, he first bought him some idlis and a cup of tea and then took him back to the building.

Perumal told the old man that he could consider recruiting him but first he wanted him to understand the terms of the contract. At the end of each day, he should hand over all the cash collected. The target for the first week would be Rs. 100, second week Rs. 200 and by the end of the month it would be Rs. 300 a week. After six months, it would be hiked to Rs. 500 a week. If he failed to achieve the targeted level by six months, some part of his body would be broken to enhance his sympathy value and thus his earning power. If he achieved and exceeded the targets consistently, he would be elevated and sent to more lucrative locations. In return he would get a place in the building to lie on and also keep his thingsand get two meals a day. In case of shortfall in the collection, one of the meals would be cut.

The devotees visiting the temple may not always give in cash, they may give in kind. If they gave the temple prasadam or sometimes biscuits and such eatables in open condition, he was welcome to eat it or share it with others. But if he received it in packed condition, he was not to open it but was to give it to Perumal. Such items were not meant for consumption but for recycling. They would go back to the shops and Perumal would get his commission. There would be no share in it for him.

Any act of cheating or unionism would render the contract void and he would be thrown out. Likewise he was not to steal anything from the public or from any of the shops. If he did so and was caught, the contract would be terminated and he would be handed over to the police. He was also forbidden from entering the temple. If he did, he would lose his contract.

If he agreed to the terms, he was welcome to stay. If not, he may leave and he need not pay for the food. Buchi Babu respected the man for his straight forward approach and appreciated him for having spelt out the terms of engagement in advance and for giving him a choice to accept or reject. He felt that the man was not bad as such and his terms too seemed to be fair enough.

If his previous employers had been even half as good as this one he would not have been driven to such dire straits. He remembered the adage 'beggars cannot be choosers'. But that came after one chose to become a beggar. He was being offered that choice. Since he did not have any other option to choose from, he agreed to the man's terms and entered into the unwritten contract of agreement.

That was how he had landed here.

Lost in his thoughts, he had closed his eyes and was half asleep. Suddenly, he heard the screeching sound of tyres, a thud and a lot of screams. Before he realized what was happening, something landed on his lap followed by the crying of a baby. He looked down to see a bundle of pink soft cushioned cloth with an even pinker baby in it crying its heart out. As he wondered where in the heavens it came from, he looked up to see all the other beggars and a whole lot of people crowded around the bend of the road with men shouting and women wailing. He found that the temple door was also being shut, though it was not yet closing time.

Involuntarily he patted the baby on the chest ever so lightly and made soothing sounds. The baby soon calmed down and stopped crying. The baby became so silent that he feared it was dead and hastily put his hand on its chest. He was relieved to note that the baby had only fallen asleep. It would wake up soon and start crying again. He had to do something.

Before he could even get up holding the baby to his chest, the police arrived and started driving people out. He had to retreat to the building before being pushed by the crowd. He made his way to the building being careful not to disturb the baby. On reaching the building, he went to his allotted slot and gently laid the baby down. The baby was not more than 4 months old.

Now he heard the sounds of others returning to the building. They were making a lot of noise as everyone seemed to be speaking animatedly. He hoped that the commotion would not wake the baby up. All of a sudden there was total silence. He looked up to see that everyone of them was staring at the baby in total astonishment and disbelief.

Before anyone could utter a word, he cautioned them to be silent and gestured to them to come out of the building. Once out of the building, he told them how he had suddenly found the baby on his lap and what happened thereafter. It was now his turn to ask them what the commotion on the road was all about. One of them narrated what had happened.

As they sat there begging, they saw a motorcycle take the bend opposite the temple entrance. As the motorcycle was turning, a car also took the bend and tried to overtake the bike. There was another vehicle coming from the opposite side. To avoid colliding with the oncoming vehicle, the car swerved to the left and hit the bike. As the car hit the bike, the girl sitting at the back was thrown off the bike and the boy and the bike got run over by the car. Both the boy and the girl died on the spot.

They inferred that as the girl got thrown off the bike, by some providence, the baby she was holding must have been thrown off her hands and landed on Buchi Babu's lap. Everyone agreed that it was a miracle. This led to a philosophical discussion on the ways of the LORD and

HIS miracles. Suddenly, one of them raised his hand and the chattering stopped. The baby was crying.

All of them scrambled back into the building. Each tried an innovative way to draw the baby's attention so that it would stop crying. Nothing seemed to work until Kamala came forward and took the baby into her arms. Her hands trembled as she gently lifted the baby up to her bosom. Her dark, dirty and scraggy arms against the extremely fair, clean and tender skin of the baby made her almost drop the baby. She felt guilty. She thought she had no right to touch the baby. She was about to put the baby back but stopped.

The baby had now stopped crying and was desperately looking to feed. How could she, a beggar woman dare to feed a baby from a well to do family? The very thought scared her. She was scared of the consequences of such an act. She was not sure whether in the first place she would be able to feed the child. Her own little boy was nearing six months and there was hardly enough for him. Yet, involuntarily she moved towards her corner with the baby which seemed desperately hungry.

The others retreated to their places in silence.

As the baby suckled hard, Kamala kept shifting the baby between her teats and cried in silence. After struggling for quite a while, the baby finally gave up, even though only half fed. The baby then dozed off on her lap. Her son too lay by her side fast asleep. He would wake up soon and cry. She shuddered at the thought.

Kamala was an orphan who was born to beg. Right from a very tender age she was inducted into the begging trade. As a child, she enjoyed her life among beggars but as she stepped into adolescence, she understood the miserable life she was leading. She used to look at all those well dressed, well fed and well cared for young girls who visited the temple with their parents and cry in silence at her fate.

As she matured into a young woman, she became scared and suspicious of everyone. Though she was malnourished and underfed, she looked pretty and charming, qualities that come naturally with youth.

Soon she was forced to get pregnant to improve her sympathy quotient and to achieve her contractual targets. As the days progressed and the fetus grew inside her, she felt an unknown joy. Each day was an experience that made her feel wonderful in some strange way. But it was taking a toll of her weak and frail body and each day she felt she may not live to see the next day. As the D day approached, she hoped she would not survive child birth but GOD willed otherwise and she survived. The post natal life felt even more miserable that at times she thought of killing herself and her infant especially when she was unable to feed him. Now suddenly, as if to add fuel to the fire, here was another child on her lap, another orphan like her.

Buchi Babu and others debated as to what they should do next and by consensus agreed that they should wait for Perumal to show up and do nothing until then. Perumal owned a tea shop cum snack bar at the end of the lane leading to the temple and abutting the main road. Through his shop he had learnt of the accident and that the temple was closed for the day. So he did not turn up at the old building until late evening.

He was shocked to see the baby and learn how it happened to be among his beggars. He shouted, screamed and abused them and even kicked a couple of them for failing to inform him. He slapped Buchi Babu and abused him for having brought the baby here. He should have approached one of the policemen on the spot and handed over the baby to the police. At least, if they had informed the cashier at the tea shop, he would have been alerted about this. He would have told them what to do or would have come down immediately and done the right thing. He feared what action the police would take if they discovered this new baby amongst his gang of beggars. It was better to go to the police station and inform them. But it was quite late in the evening to do so. He therefore decided to postpone it to the next morning and hoped nothing happened overnight.

When he learnt that Kamala was unable to feed the baby and the baby was starving, he cursed her and kicked her. He didn't want the baby to die of starvation. That was the last thing he wanted. So he took Buchi Babu to the tea shop and arranged for some milk and also bought a feeding bottle from one of the shops on the main road.

So the baby was back to Buchi's corner. The baby drank the milk happily and dozed off much to the relief of all. Soon every one fell asleep and lost themselves in their dreams. It was about 1.00 when they were all jolted back out of their deep sleep. It took a short while for them to realize what had woken them up. The baby was crying again. As there was no milk left, Buchi stuck the empty feeding bottle into its mouth but the baby pushed it away.

It was again Kamala who came forward. The baby had soiled the diaper. She deftly removed it and after cleaning up the mess and washing the baby and her dress, put her to sleep. Since there was no spare dress for the child, she was wrapped in Buchi's banian. The baby slept and the night passed without further events.

Chapter 2

AT THE STATION

Perumal and Buchi Babu went to the Korukkupettai police station by 8.00 am so as to meet the Circle Inspector Sundarapandian, Station House Officer (SHO) as soon as he arrived. They did not take the baby with them. As soon as Palanichamy, the Assistant Sub Inspector (ASI) saw them, he became a little apprehensive as Perumal was not supposed to come to the station unless called. The ASI was the one who visited Perumal regularly to collect the mamool (bribe).

He took them aside and asked quite acidly what they were doing at the station. Perumal narrated the incidents of the previous day and Buchi kept nodding his head appropriately. They did not like the look on Palanichamy's face as he heard their story.

Palanichamy felt very uncomfortable as he was the one who had filed the First Information Report (FIR), copies of which were filed with the Mortuary along with the challan for transfer of the bodies and with the charge sheet sent to the Magistrate's office for proceeding against the negligent driver and with the comprehensive investigation report sent to the office of the Superintendent of Police (SP).

More importantly, none of the reports made any mention of the existence of the baby.

So he told them to wait somewhere away from the station and that he would call them as soon as the SHO was in and apprised of the matter.

Perumal again abused and scolded Buchi for not using his head and for acting like an idiot putting him in unwanted trouble. Buchi bore it in silence and did not try to justify his actions. He could see that Perumal was getting worked up and did not want to make it worse by saying something that may seem inappropriate or infuriating to Perumal.

By 10.30 or so, the ASI gestured to them to come. They hastened to the station. Perumal asked Buchi to stay outside and went with the ASI to the SHO's room. Sundarapandian normally bullied people and Perumal knew it only too well having been given the 'works' on a few occasions. Surprisingly the SHO greeted Perumal and enquired quite sweetly what this was all about. Perumal narrated the story again, though a little hastily. He feared the SHO may lose patience suddenly.

Buchi Babu was called in. One look at him and Sundarapandian knew that he was not a 'beggar'. He wanted to know how he came to be in Perumal's gang. But he did not pursue any enquiry in that direction. He only asked Buchi to narrate the incident in his words.

After hearing them out, he asked Buchi what he wanted to do with the baby. Buchi promptly said that he wanted the baby to be handed over to the family to which it belonged. The SHO casually asked Buchi what if the family didn't want the baby. This was totally unexpected and it was quite baffling even to think about such a thing. He blinked and looked at Perumal, who was doing the same thing and looking at Buchi. They just didn't know what to say.

Sundarapandian understood their predicament quite well. He then told them that the baby's parents belonged to different faiths and they had married against the wishes of their parents and families. On being informed of the accident and their death, the parents of both the boy and the girl had said that they didn't care because to them they were already dead. They were not coming forward to claim anything that belonged to them, not even their bodies.

Their employers were informed of the position and they offered to take possession of the belongings of the deceased and settle dues. The SHO told them that under the circumstances it was unlikely anyone would come forward to take care of the baby especially a baby girl. He also made it clear that he was unwilling to alter any of his records in the absence of a claimant for the baby.

Further, he said that it was not advisable to keep the baby in their joint. It was too risky. Anyone may spot the child, become suspicious, take a photograph of the baby in the hands of a beggar or among beggars and post it on the social media network. It will definitely go viral. If that happened, there would be trouble for him and his staff and Perumal and his gang.

So he strongly advised Perumal to take the baby out of that place immediately and move it to any other place. He could either keep it in his own house or at any of his employee's place. But the best option may be to leave it outside an orphanage.

As they were contemplating on his idea, he commented that something that was bothering him since yesterday had become clear now. They blinked again and wondered what he was going to say next.

The Police had retrieved from the accident site a pink bag that contained a lot of baby things. He had not included that in his report believing that someone in the crowd might have dropped it amidst all the chaos that prevailed immediately after that accident. Another reason why he thought so was that the bag was lying quite far from the body of the girl whereas her handbag was lying quite close to the spot of the accident.

He told the ASI to give that bag to them. Taking cue that they had been dismissed, Perumal and Buchi started to leave with the ASI. Sundarapandian asked them to wait. When ASI Palanichamy came back with the pink bag, he asked him to hand it over to Buchi Babu. He then dismissed the ASI. He detained Buchi and told Perumal to come back after an hour. Perumal was too confused to think straight. So he felt quite relieved when asked to leave but felt very uncomfortable about Buchi's detention.

When they were alone, Sundarapandian came straight to the point and asked Buchi how he came to be amongst Perumal's beggars. Buchi felt a strange comfort in the company of this man who was otherwise quite overpowering both physically and mentally. So he told his story.

Buchi Babu secured a job as a Clerical Assistant in a private concern in Tondiarpet soon after school. Though the salary wasn't much, he enjoyed working in the concern. The founder employer was kind, compassionate and treated his employees well, especially those who worked well and were useful to the organization. Buchi Babu found plenty of opportunity to learn and to prove his worth to the organization. The management exploited such workers with kind words and compassionate gestures. When it came to money matters, all workers were equal. So while Buchi and his likes toiled hard, the less loyal ones enjoyed.

Buchi did not mind. In the comfort of his job, he married and soon had a son. With the meager salary on the one hand and the responsibilities of a married man with a family on the other, Buchi struggled hard to make both ends meet but never sacrificed moral values. He tried to live with dignity within his means. So he maintained a lean family of one child and no more.

As times changed and businesses diversified, the management too changed. Buchi was among the few loyalists left. The others had retired or died while the not so loyalists either set up their own business or left for greener pastures. Some stayed on to exploit the management. The respect Buchi had enjoyed earlier had also waned. He was being kept for old times' sake, though he had adapted himself to changing times and upgraded his skills to continue to be useful to the organization. Meanwhile his son had become a bully and a tartar, spoilt by his doting mother. But education wise he was not bad. He was above average, though not in the 'good' category.

As his son graduated somehow and secured a job in an IT related industry, he started earning more than Buchi did after 25 years of service. They soon got him married to an educated girl who also earned more than Buchi did.

Meanwhile, at work, the management changed yet again and passed on to the next generation. Buchi found himself working under a boss younger than his son. Everything at the work place had changed, which had no room for old fashioned ideas like ethics and loyalty. The ends were more important than the means. Buchi found it more and more difficult to adapt himself to such changes most of which were against his conscience.

On the home front, Buchi lost his wife and with her went his status of 'Head' of the family. The son who became the new 'Head' treated him with scant respect and tolerated him only for the 'money' he brought as his wages, which in the eyes of his son were peanuts. Yet money was money. Buchi had to give his entire wages to his son and would in return receive two meals a day, minimal clothing and shelter under his roof. The son had turned into a tyrant.

A month ago, his boss had unceremoniously sacked him as he was found to be no longer useful to the organization. On learning of the loss of job and the meager earnings, his son had thrown him out of the house. His daughter-in-law tried to plead for him. She was told to leave with him if she loved him so much. She immediately backed out too scared to say anything more.

Buchi felt too devastated to go to anyone else when his own son had discarded him like waste. He wandered for a couple of days seeking petty jobs but in vain. When he felt too tired to continue, he had taken shelter under Perumal, who was at least better than his previous employer.

Sundarapandian was all sympathy for Buchi. The SHO was not only a kind person but also pious. He was a different man only when in uniform. After a long silence, he asked Buchi whether he didn't see a Divine hand behind all the events. Buchi did not really understand and only managed to blink.

Sundarapandian lamented that the problem with people in general was that they viewed life in small compartments and never looked at the larger picture. He then asked Buchi to see it from the perspective of the life of the baby girl. The baby's parents were destined to die but not the baby. Since the baby's parents were outcasts, neither family would take care of the baby. But the baby's care was to be entrusted to someone kind and responsible. God chose Buchi for the task and had to get him to the place to be available to receive the baby when the time arrived. So he first made him jobless, then homeless and finally hopeless so that he would be where God wanted him to be when the time came.

Buchi protested and said that God could not have entrusted the care of the baby to a hopeless wretch like him. Sundarapandian pacified him and asked him not to worry but to have faith in God. He then told Buchi that everything had fallen in place as per God's will and it was now Sundarapandian's turn to do what was expected of him.

He then picked up the phone and made a call to someone. He told him that he wanted to see him regarding an urgent matter and that he would be there in an hour. He thanked the person and called off. Buchi saw nothing but bleakness ahead but this man seemed quite confident. Buchi had always feared God but never really worshipped. To him work was worship.

The ASI knocked and informed that Perumal was back. The SHO called him in. Perumal was relieved to see that Buchi was in one piece. The SHO told Perumal to go and buy some decent clothes for Buchi. This unexpected order confused Perumal and he stood blinking. Sundarapandian realized that he should explain. So he told Perumal that Buchi would no longer be part of his gang. He wanted him relieved and as settlement, he wanted Perumal to give Buchi new clothes – Dhoties, Shirts and innerwear. He also told him to get some toiletries and a towel as well. Buchi would bring up the child as per God's will and that Sundarapandian would do his bit.

Perumal knew that he could not cross swords with this man. If the SHO decided something, the wisest thing was to agree with him. So, if that is what he wanted that is what Perumal would do. He made haste and returned soon with new clothes and toiletries for Buchi Babu.

Sundarapandian called Palanichamy and asked him to take Buchi to a paid public convenience nearby so that he could wash and change into the new clothes. When the SHO told Perumal about his plans for Buchi and the baby, Perumal felt relieved. He had never been comfortable with Buchi. Despite the rags, unshaven face, unclean and unkempt hair, the man's dignity came through even in his body language. So he had asked Buchi to keep his head down while begging and never to look into anyone's eyes. In short, Buchi really didn't fit in and the SHO had seen it at first glance. Perumal had been more worried about the baby than Buchi. The SHO's plans relieved him of both of them.

Chapter 3

AT THE HOME

Buchi Babu was hurrying back from work. He was already late by half an hour. Shankari would have returned from school and would be eagerly waiting for him at the 'home'. He was eager to tell her that they would be soon moving into a residence of their own.

He wondered how soon the last five years had fled. With the blessings of the SHO Sundarapandian, he had moved into a 'home' for destitute children in Teynampet with his infant girl. Though the pink bag and other things in the bag carried the name Sweety, the SHO and the Siva Temple Trustee Manickavasagam had decided on the name Shankari for the baby girl as it was outside the Siva Temple that she had come into their lives. The Trustee who also ran the Teynampet home for destitute children readily agreed to put them up there.

It was a good move. The young Shankari was always surrounded by children who doted on her and adored her like a Goddess given her angelic looks and complexion. So Buchi got the all essential food, shelter and company to raise the child. He was also given a job in one of Manickavasagam's businesses. The man was in textiles, readymade garments, granites and other mineral exports. Buchi was assigned a job in the export business. He worked hard and did overtime and also worked part time at other places on his weekly day off to try and save as much as possible for the child's future.

In the course of his job, he had met Haji Janab Gulam Ali Saheb, the founder and owner of the Noor-e-Islam Empire. The empire had under its roof agencies for liners, freight forwarding, custom house and companies involved in trading, transport, warehousing and cold storage. The Haji was highly respected and regarded in official, social, political and religious circles as a man of high virtues and wisdom. The Haji had a Man Friday Salam Mohammed, who suddenly left for the heavenly abode leaving the Haji in a dilemma to find a replacement for him. When he was looking for a man to take his place, he remembered Buchi and spoke to Manickavasagam about sparing him. Manickavasagam readily agreed and asked Buchi to go and see the Haji without telling him why.

When Buchi met the Haji, he told him about his conversation with Manickavasagam and offered Buchi Salam's job at a salary which was three times more than what he was being paid by Manickavasagam. The Haji further offered him as perks a rented flat and a handsome allowance for the child's education. The offer could not be refused.

Buchi realized that though the 'home' provided a safe and secure shelter, it was time for the child to grow up in a different environment, a home of its own. The single bed room flat he had rented in Royapettah in a large complex housing several flats could be a little small for a growing child but she would certainly not feel lonely as there were several families with children surrounding the flat he had chosen.

On reaching the 'home' he distributed sweets and told the inmates of his new job and the flat they would be moving into. The initial joy soon faded as they felt very sad that Shankari would no longer be with them. Some cried and some protested but in the end they all understood that it was inevitable.

The day of parting turned out to be highly emotional and quite challenging. On moving into the new house, they felt quite lonely and missed all the children at the 'home'. Shankari cried and wanted to go back to the home.

But soon, she got used to the new surroundings and her school. It was quite a daunting task for Buchi to play the roles of a bread winner and a home maker and bring up a child on his own. Shankari became the darling of her classmates at school as well as neighbours at home. She was such a sweet child that one could not help but love her. She was also brilliant in her studies and had a sharp mind that grasped everything fast. She had a sweet voice too. One of the neighbours who ran a music and dance school took her in as one of her students and was amazed at the pace at which she learnt and mastered the arts.

As an infant she had called him 'baba'. It sounded so sweet that he encouraged her to call him that. The others at the 'home' too started calling him Baba. He liked it because it was definitely better than thatha or uncle and it also gave him a new identity.

He continued to be called Baba at the new place too.

He didn't know Shankari's date of birth. So the day she came into his life was celebrated as her birthday. Every year on her birthday, he took her to the Siva Temple and offered prayers in her name and distributed food packets to his beggar friends. Then he would take her to meet the SHO and then Manickavasagam. Now after moving into the new place, a visit to the 'home' was included.

The visits had a lasting effect on the girl particularly after she turned 4. She asked him a lot of questions. He answered cleverly in a way a child of her age would understand that evoked sympathy and compassion for them in the girl's heart.

On her 6th birthday when they visited the temple, they learnt that Kamala had died leaving her son Manikandanan orphan. With the help of the SHO and the blessings of Manickavasagam, Buchi got the boy shelter in the Teynampet 'home'.

Shankari did exceedingly well in her academics as well as in co curricular activities at the school. After school, she played with other children in the apartments, and at home she started assisting Buchi in the house hold chores. Before going to bed she would read aloud stories from Chandamama and he would explain to her the stories and the morals behind them. Sometimes she would doze off half way through.

As they went through the motions of their busy lives, time seemed to race at a furious pace.

Chapter 4

FIRST LESSONS

It was raining very heavily and flooding the whole city. It was a welcome relief after months of scorching heat. The candle light flickered in the breeze that had squeezed through the gaps in the windows and threw up ghostly shadows on the wall.

Baba was not yet home. She wondered where he was. She knew that his umbrella would be of no use in this weather. So she had kept a set of dry clothes and a towel ready for him. She had also warmed the milk and the decoction so that when he changed into dry clothes she could offer him a cup of hot coffee.

While on the one hand she was anxious for her Baba's safe return and kept thinking of him, on the other hand her thoughts involuntarily reverted to the fascinating experience she had felt as she had watched the senior girls rehearsing for a dance drama performance they were to make soon. They were the students of her music teacher who resided in another block of the apartment complex. She had felt strangely drawn to the sheer magic of the song and the tune it was setto. She was thrilled by the experience – the joy of watching the girls dance so gracefully and exhibiting emotions she did not quite understand. She felt she understood, yet she found that she did not really.

At the end of the rehearsal, she had asked her teacher to explain what it was. The teacher had merely patted her on the back and said sweetly that she would understand in course of time, meaning she was too young to understand. Shankari felt a little offended. But she loved and adored her teacher so much that she accepted it for a fact. After all, her 10th birthday was still a few months away.

As the rain lashed heavily to the accompaniment of thunder and lightning, she grew more and more anxious. Then to her relief, Buchi knocked on the door and called out to her. She ran to the door and opened it. He was totally drenched and was dripping from top to toe. She took the wet bag and the umbrella from his hands, kept them on the floor near the door and fetched the dry towel she had kept for him. By the time he changed into dry clothes, she brought him a cup of hot coffee. He was touched by her concern and sense of responsibility and overcome with joy. He kept the coffee down, hugged her and planted a kiss on her forehead.

As he sat sipping the hot coffee she told him about the dance rehearsal. He promised to take her to the hall to see the performance on stage which was scheduled for the following Sunday. After about an hour when the rains subsided, power was restored. After supper as the girl slept peacefully, Buchi looked back on his life. He realized how right Sundarapandian was. He admired him for his strong and unshakable faith and belief in God. The child was truly blessed. He was taking care of every step of her life. The journey so far was nothing less than miraculous. He wondered what was in store for the future and admitted to himself that he lacked the wisdom and vision of Sundarapandian.

On Sunday they were seated in the Kamarajar Arangam to enjoy watching the dance drama 'Thillaiar Thiru Ula' produced, directed and choreographed by her music teacher Gomati Narayanan, who had arranged for special passes for them.

The show started with a brief introduction by the Director herself. The drama depicted the procession of Thillai Natarajar in Chidambaram and the effect the Lord has on women of different age groups. The Ula is based on a song sung by Cheraman Perumal Nayanar in the 8th Century AD in which he touched upon the seven stages of a woman found in ancient Tamil Literature.The song adapted to the dance drama was set to music composed by her Guru. She went on to briefly explain the techniques adopted by her and then followed it up with an introduction of the dancers, singers and accompanying artists on various instruments.

The show opened to a grand spectacle of the deity Lord Nataraja leaving the temple for a grand procession of the streets around the temple. As the Lord entered the street, a young and innocent child, a Pedai[3] meets the procession. She is overwhelmed by the grandeur of the deity decked in colourful flowers and sparkling jewelry. She is wonderstruck and takes in the spectacle in joyous wonder. She is attracted to the deity with a spontaneous innocence and childish joy.

As the Lord moves forward, another girl, a Pedumbai[4], who is equally attracted to the deity but with a sense of wonder meets the Lord. She feels immense joy and a sense of awakening within her which she is able to experience but unable to comprehend. She is drawn to the deity and his overpowering beauty and sees herself in relation to the Lord without knowing what exactly it is.

3 Pedai – age 5–7, a naïve and innocent girl.

4 Pedumbai – age 8–11, an adolescent girl, one who understands yet does not.

As the procession takes a bend, there is yet another girl, a Mangai[5], who instantly falls in love with the Lord. She too is overwhelmed by the beauty of the Lord and his divine form. She feels and experiences an emotion of love within her but without an understanding of the intricacies of love. She experiences a joy in the strange relationship and oneness with God.

The procession of the Lord moves on and now attracts the attention of a young woman, a Madandai[6], who not only falls in love but takes a bold step and approaches her Lord. She is aware of her aesthetic love and acts in that awareness. She imagines the Lord to be her Hero.

Further on, the Lord now attracts an adult woman, Arivai[7], who is knowledgeable and has a deeper understanding of herself. She is focused in her devotion and love towards her Lord. Besides love, she feels other attendant emotions such as desire, excitement, awe and even a certain jealousy towards other women and a certain passion arising out of devotion.

As the Lord's procession proceeds round the temple, there is now a mature woman, Therivai[8], who is not clouded by passion but is focused on her devotion to the Lord. She is clear in her understanding of the grace of the Lord and her relationship with him as His devotee.

As the Lord takes the last bend to return to the temple, there is a more mature woman, a Perilampenn[9], who has risen

5 Mangai – age 12–13, a maiden, one who has stepped into early adulthood.

6 Madandai – age 14–19, a young woman whose heart keeps fluttering.

7 Arivai – age 20–25, a knowledgeable young woman of marriable age.

8 Therivai – age 25–31, a mature woman, who can take rational decisions.

9 Perilampenn – age 32–40, a fully mature woman.

above 'self' and in sublime devotion, has surrendered herself to her Lord. She seeks only refuge in Him.

As the Lord reenters the temple, the curtains came down bringing the spectacular show to an end.

The spellbound audience stood up and clapped in roaring applause. Shankari was thrilled beyond words and clapped gleefully as Buchi too joined her with joy.

They went into the green room and congratulated her teacher and the dancers on a wonderful and riveting performance. Shankari hugged and kissed them. She would cherish this experience for a long time. All the way back home and at home, she spoke endlessly. He was very pleased to see her so happy.

As she kept talking about it now and then in the days that followed, Buchi felt it was the right time to prepare the child for her future. So one day he sat down with her after supper and told her that there were three important turning points in the life of a woman. She became all ears.

The three turning points are marked by life changing events, First Blood, First Child and the Last Blood.

The first turning point is when a girl turns into a woman. He explained to her the hormonal changes that occur in the body and start preparing a girl for the future event of child bearing. When she showed some fear and concern about bleeding, he calmed her by saying it lasts only for three days every month and after about 100 cycles during which the girl grows physically and mentally strong, she is ready for the next event, the first child.

The second event turns the woman into a mother, a gift of God. The experience of carrying and nurturing a life within is a marvelous experience and one which makes a woman special. Then when she delivers a child, it gives rise to the birth of the child and the mother. That is why they say at child birth, the woman has a rebirth. It changes her life entirely and makes her a new person altogether. She may have more children but by then she is already a mother. So it is not the same as the first child.

She continues to have her cycles but after about another 150 to 200 cycles, it stops. With the last cycle, her child bearing life comes to an end. A woman of that age invariably suffers from emotional and physical problems during that time as she feels that it is the end of her life. But sooner or later she recovers and realizes that she has completed a full circle and become a girl again. She can now enjoy the freedom she enjoyed as a girl. The burden of being a woman is no longer there.

Many women may miss or skip the middle event but no woman can escape the first and the last. They are part of being a woman.

Shankari took keen interest in what he told her and in the end said quite seriously that the most important stages are then the Mangai and the Arivai. He was amazed at the way she related it so well to what she had witnessed in the dance drama.

Note: Sangam literature divides the life of women into seven stages. They are Pedai (first 5 years), Pedumai (5–10 years), Mangai (10–16 years), Madanthai (16–25 years), Arivai (25–45 years), Therivai (45–60 years), Perilampenn (above 60 years).

Chapter 5

LAURELS

The Auditorium of R.K Senior Secondary School was packed to the full. A special function was organized to felicitate the students who had excelled in their Secondary and Senior Secondary Board Exams and made the School proud.

After the customary speeches by the Subject Teachers and the Principal, the students were felicitated.

First, every student who had scored a centum was called to the stage and given a memento and a 'certificate of appreciation' from the school to the resounding applause from the fellow students.

Next it was the turn of the school toppers in each subject followed by those who had obtained state ranks.

In the end the school topper and one of the top three State Rankers, Shankari, was called to the stage. As she moved forward, the claps started and rose in a crescendo. She went up the stage, touched the feet of the Principal, the Correspondent, other elders on the stage and then the Chief Guest before receiving the memento from him.

She was called upon to speak. As she took the mike, the hall fell silent. She spoke highly of her teachers and the school without whose relentless efforts she could not have achieved such distinction. She said she owed her future to them and that she would always remember them at every walk of life.

She then said she owed her life to her Baba. She said what she had achieved was not her achievement but that of her Baba and revealed the story of her life. So she dedicated the achievement to her Baba who was God to her. Her speech moved everyone to tears. So when she thanked God for giving her Baba and bowed out of the stage, there was pin drop silence. Soon the crowd recovered and the hall filled with the sound of claps that never seemed to stop.

As she came down the stage and touched his feet, Buchi Babu was overcome with emotion. No words would come out. So he just touched her head and blessed her.

The days ahead were busy days. After perusing all the options and consulting her well wishers and patrons, the Haji, Manickavasagam and Sundarapandian, they chose Vaishnava College to pursue a course of her choice in 'Media and Communication'.

Once the course started Shankari became busy with her academics, projects, field trips, interviews with stars and celebrities, writing articles for dailies, weeklies and online magazines besides participating in all arts and cultural events.

She had made a lot of friends and a host of admirers for her beauty, intelligence, modest behavior, dignified manners, and eloquence in speech and thought-provoking and compassionate articles.

She pursued in parallel her passion for music and dance under her beloved Gomati teacher. Her life was on a roller coaster and poor old Buchi tried to keep pace amidst his own hectic schedule at work and at home.

Amongst her many admirers, there was one boy Buchi liked. He was Trilochan, the only son of a well educated and well placed couple from Andhra, who had settled in Chennai. While the father was a Senior Auditor in Defence Accounts, the mother was a Director in the Accountant General's office. They lived in the same complex but in a much larger 3 Bedroom flat. The boy was about five years older than Shankari and as a young Chartered Accountant had joined a leading private firm with a large clientele.

Trilochan was one of the regulars at Gomati teacher's school. He too was a good dancer, though he never graduated to perform on the stage. He and Shankari were good friends. He accompanied her to music concerts and dance performances whenever Buchi could not find time to do so. Buchi did not mind sending the girl with this boy.

The boy would drop in at home and chat with them and likewise Shankari would visit his parents at times. She was the boy's mother's favourite. They would chat on and on endlessly. His father too would often discussher studies, college and her articles. In short, his parents liked her and did not mind their friendship.

In course of time, a fondness developed between them, which did not go unnoticed. Both Buchi and Trilochan's parents thought they made a good pair. But they themselves did not realize it as such, caught up in their busy lives as they were. While Shankari was busy with her academic and cultural pursuits, Trilochan was busy building his career.

She continued to maintain high performance levels at college as at school. Though she had a tougher competition and lesser time on hand, she managed to occupy the top slot in rankings.

Buchi Babu after sharing his thoughts with his boss and his two well-wishers and learning of their approval to his proposal approached Trilochan's parents with some apprehension. After some initial hesitation, he discussed a possible alliance for his girl with their son. The conversation turned pleasant when he learnt that they too were thinking on the same lines. In the end they agreed to allow the matter to rest for now and wait to see what the girl and the boy had to say. They also decided not to broach the subject until her graduation was complete.

Her graduation was coming to an end. It was just a couple of months away.

An inter-collegiate dance competition was also coming to a close with the finals just a week ahead. The organizers of the competition had adopted a unique technique to conduct the competition. First they sent out invitations to various colleges for registration of entries. Next they called for a concept document on the theme chosen and short listed the entries for the next stage on that basis. In the third stage the competing colleges were asked to organize a presentation of their dance within their college premises. This was attended by the judges nominated by the organizers. The judges chose the top three for a final showdown at a private hall.

The three finalist colleges would present their dance to last not more than 20 minutes each with two 10 minute breaks in between. While one college had chosen Kalidasa's Shakuntala, the second had chosen the divine love of Radha and Krishna and Shankari's college had chosen Dakshayani as their theme. The organizers appointed 100 judges who would be seated among the audience and each was to choose just one of the three performances in the end and communicate the same through SMS using a onetime password. The top team would get the prize. If there was a tie the prize would be shared.

On the day of the competition, as the clock struck six, the first show began with Menaka enchanting sage Vishwamitra leading to the birth of Shakuntala. Then followed the story of how she was abandoned and found by sage Kanva, how she grew up in the hermitage Tapovan into a beautiful woman and how King Dushyanta happened to come across her. Then followed scenes of their romance and the gifting of the ring, the curse of sage Durvasa, the loss of the ring, Dushyanta's failure to recognize her plunging her into sorrow, the dramatic finding of the ring and Dushyanta's return to the Tapovan to take his wife and his prince. The girl who played Shakuntala stole the show exhibiting a range of emotions alternating between extreme joy and extreme sorrow. The others too complemented her very well to make the show captivating.

The next show was equally good in every aspect and was very interesting as the artists who played Radha and Krishna competed with each other to make the show excellent. Their outstanding performance combined with the lovely settings and scintillating background score made it tough for the judges to choose between the two performances.

As the curtains rose for the third and the last show against a narrative in the background, the audience were treated to a grand spectacle of the yaga being performed by Dakhsa to which Lord Siva was intentionally not invited. Despite being told by Siva not to, Dakshayani goes to the palace of her father uninvited. She questions her father how he could perform the yaga without inviting Lord Siva. The arrogant Daksha mocks and humiliates her and this leads to explosive arguments between the father and the daughter. In the end, unable to bear the insults and the humiliation, Dakshayani jumps into the fire and sacrifices her life.

The setting changed here and a solo performance by Shankari began.

Having got rid of her mortal form, Shakti rises to Kailash and admits to Siva her folly and asks for forgiveness. Siva refuses to accept her. This leads to another serious argument and tempers start flying high culminating in a ferocious dance, the Siva Thandavam. Alternating between Siva and Shakthi, Shankari started dancing like one possessed. By now she had taken the stage by storm. She felt as though she was becoming one with her Lord Siva. She felt her energy fast drying up.

Then to restore peace on earth Brahma and Vishnu appear and appeal to the cosmic couple to stop the Thandavam. The couple realizes that peace lies only in their union and thus unites to form Ardhanareeswarar.

Ardhanareeswarar

At this point, the stage turned dark except for a spot light on Shankari with an image of Ardhanareeswarar super imposed on her. The dancer had transformed and the audience was stunned. It made them feel as though they were in the presence of the Lord and His Consort themselves. As the audience was still dazed, the lights went out plunging the hall into total darkness. Shankari felt darkness engulfing and consuming her. The curtain immediately fell and the lights returned.

Behind the curtain fellow artists rushed to the stage to congratulate Shankari but were shocked to see her lying unconscious on the floor. She had stopped breathing. They immediately lifted her and took her to the green room. The girls started crying and the teachers were too confused by the turn of events as no one had expected such a tragic end to the performance. People started making frantic calls for ambulance and doctors.

Engulfed in total darkness for a while, Shankari found a faint light far away which started growing gradually and soon surrounded her lulling her into a blissful peace. Suddenly, as gradually as it had started, the light which had engulfed her, started fading and the darkness returned.

Someone had found a doctor who was examining her. As she was doing so, Shankari started breathing slowly and then coughed and woke up much to everyone's relief and joy. As she sat up and enquired what had happened, the doctor told her there was nothing to worry. Everything was normal. It must have been due to exhaustion and suggested some fresh fruit juice. Soon the girls hugged and kissed her in joy.

The strange phenomenon she had experienced gave her a sense of peace and wisdom. So she was quite calm and composed when she rose and joined the team. She felt rejuvenated and recharged. The team mates were surprised to see her so very energetic as hardly ten minutes earlier she had been lying unconscious.

The girls were now jumping in joy as their team had won hands down. The other teams too came and congratulated Shankari on the wonderful performance. They acknowledged that it was par excellence and deserved to win.

Congratulations kept pouring in for the next one week as the newspapers and magazines that reported the event went overboard in praising her performance.

Shankari was not affected by all the accolades. She started preparing seriously for her final year examinations. It was during this time, that the campus interviews were also held. She was offered the job of an Assistant Editor in one of the leading dailies to which she contributed articles regularly. She was excited about the offer and Buchi felt very happy. She informed Trilochan and his parents too. It was then that Trilochan proposed to her. Though she felt very pleased, she did not show it and said she wanted to let it lie till her exams were over. He understood that she wanted to first talk to her Baba and get his approval before giving her consent. So he just smiled and said he would wait.

The exams were over and the results were awaited. She had become relatively free. It was then that she told Buchi about Trilochan's proposal. He readily gave his consent and told her to inform Trilochan without delay. Meanwhile Trilochan informed his parents and took their consent. Now Buchi moved fast. He arranged for their engagement without wasting any time.

Within a week of their engagement, her call letter came from the publisher to join immediately. Suddenly everything seemed to have gathered momentum.

Shankari and Trilochan visited the Siva temple and offered prayers and followed it up with distributing sweets among the beggars and the children at the 'home'. Manikandan, Kamla's son was now working as a mechanic in a fabrication unit. He was very happy to receive them and thanked them for visiting his room that he shared with a couple of colleagues at the work place.

Shankari reported for duty and was assigned to the team responsible for editing articles and reports to be published in the week-end supplements. The job was quite taxing but at the same time very interesting. During the course of the first month of her job, her results came out and she had secured the top rank in college too.

The day she received her first salary, she sought permission to leave early. She went home and was pleasantly surprised to see that her Baba too had returned early and was waiting for her. When she gave the pay cheque to him and touched his feet, they were both blinded by tears of joy and were overwhelmed with emotions.

He asked her to place the cheque at God's feet in the prayer room and take His blessings. She said that to her, he was God and that she had just done that. He told her not to be silly and asked her to do as told. When she came back, they sat and chatted for over an hour.

Then they freshened up and went to Trilochan's place. After the usual teasing and laughing, they all set out to celebrate the occasion by dining out.

It was quite late by the time they returned. Yet they did not go to bed immediately as their stomachs and hearts were full. They sat and chatted for a long time on their life's journey so far. He told her of Sundarapandian's belief that everything is pre-destined and all events just fall in place as per God's will and His grand plans. He told her that he had found it difficult to believe that, but sometimes thinking in retrospect felt that he may after all be right.

Then the topic shifted to Trilochan and his parents. He told her that he liked them for they were good people who were upright, honest, simple, God-fearing and also quite kind and compassionate. He was happy that she liked them and understood them well.

As he spoke, she stretched out on the sofa with her head on his lap. As the night wore on, she dozed off. Not wanting to disturb her he stopped chattering and lost himself in thoughts of the past when as a child she would sleep like this with her head on his lap. Slowly he too drifted into deep sleep sitting on the sofa.

At the stroke of 6.00 the next morning, Shankari woke up and was surprised to find herself on the sofa. She then saw her Baba who was still sleeping with his mouth open. She felt bad that she had made him sit the whole night. As she touched him to ask him to lie down for a while, he slumped. She panicked and tried frantically to wake him up but in vain. She called Trilochan and kept crying without uttering a word. Asking her to calm down, he enquired what had happened. She managed to control her sobs for a second and just said, "My God is no more." He immediately understood and rushed to her place with his parents.

Having served his purpose, Buchi Babu had left for his heavenly abode. It was now their turn to look after the God's child.

THE HAND OF FATE

JP, short for Jayaprakash, was just out of prison. He had nowhere to go. So he just loitered around places familiar to him looking for something to do. After loitering for a day without getting anywhere, he decided to turn over a new leaf and earn a living. So he went about searching for a job. But he found that there were no jobs for his skills – petty crimes - and for jobs available, he had no skills.

Three days of loitering left him penniless and starved. He was now desperate to do something. It was then that he chanced upon an old acquaintance Kabali. JP hoped that something would come out of this meeting. His hopes were shattered when he learnt that Kabali was in a similar fix, if not worse. But then JP was happy that at least now he had company and a partner. Together they tried to hunt for some work but in vain.

Another acquaintance from the past, Chikku, who was no better off, found them and joined them. This guy was a mobile encyclopedia of petty criminals in town. He was also a chatter box, half wit and a wise cracker. In short, he was someone who anyone would want to get rid of any day. JP and Kabali by now knew of every petty criminal and where each one was.

JP, who was by now tired, hungry and getting desperate, caught Chikku by the throat and told him to rest his tongue inside his mouth or he would cut it off for safe keeping the same in his pocket. Realizing that JP meant what he said, Chikku shut his trap and just followed them everywhere like a faithful dog.

When they were resting under a tree bereft of ideas and not knowing what to do, Chikku sought permission to speak. When granted, he said he could rope in 'idea king' Mano, who was anyway not doing anything. That gave them no hope. Yet JP said ok.

After about an hour or so, Chikku returned with Mano tagging along.

They debated for quite a while and finally decided that life inside the prison was far better than outside because you didn't have to worry about food. Some food was better than none. It was for this precise reason that the prison was full and there were not enough prisons for all. In other words, it was not easy getting in either.

So they asked Mano to think up something they could do that would land them in the prison. Now the pressure was on Mano. He had to live up to his reputation as 'idea king', though his ideas never got him or anybody else for that matter anywhere.

The lamp on Mano's thinking cap lit up and he said he had a bright idea that would work. In those days, i.e., mid 1960s, it was a crime to gamble in public and was punishable with imprisonment. It was a good idea but to implement the idea, they needed in the first place a pack of cards. Kabali asked them to leave it to him and he set off.

They waited and waited but there was no sign of Kabali. When they were ready to give up on him, they saw him walking back triumphantly and waving a 'thumbs up' sign. The next hurdle was a policeman. They needed a policeman to spot them gambling in public so that he could arrest them.

They went to several public places, not that there were many in those days, but could not find a policeman, much to their woes. Finally when they came to the town bus stand, they spotted a policeman in the distance. So they immediately set out playing cards and made enough noise to attract the attention of the policeman.

On seeing the policeman approaching them, their hopes soared. He came and stood behind them and watched them in silence. The quartet was getting nervous and wondered why the idiot was not acting. At last to their great relief he tapped his baton on Kabali's shoulder and asked them to get up. He demanded to know what they were doing. Surprised by his question, Mano asked him if he was blind. Didn't he see that they were gambling in public? He challenged the policeman to arrest them, if he dared. He was trying to provoke the idiotic policeman, who they feared may not bite the bait otherwise.

The policeman responded by asking them what the stakes were and confused them. Kabali said two rupees, a lot of money those days. The policeman said he wanted to see and asked them to take out the money. Each took out a 50 paise coin. The policeman took the two rupees, pocketed it and quietly walked away leaving the quartet looking foolish and two rupees down.

After blaming each other and hurling abuses at the policeman, they calmed down and concluded that the crime was too petty and hence did not yield a positive result. They had to think up something more substantial.

Kabali suggested that stealing could be a better option. What to steal was the next question. Those days women did not travel alone much and even if they did, they were careful not to wear or carry anything valuable. The handbag culture had not yet set in. Mano came up with the bright idea that a bicycle could be an ideal thing to steal. That was the only transport people of some affluence among the middle class owned. It was still a luxury to own a bicycle. So, stealing one could perhaps land them in the prison.

So they went hunting for a bicycle to steal. To their dismay they found that it was a heavily guarded property. All the bicycles they found were securely chained to either the Iron Gate or the wire fence and locked with a heavy padlock. It thus turned out that stealing a bicycle was not all that easy. They were thoroughly disheartened and exhausted and were losing hope of making it back to the prison. Then Chikku spotted a cycle some distance away that was neither chained nor locked. It was leaning on the gate post which itself was leaning like the Tower of Pisa. They made haste to take a closer look and were relieved to find that it was indeed neither chained nor locked.

Now, having targeted the cycle, they had to wait for a witness who would report the event and give a description of the quartet. After an anxious ten minutes, a young man showed up on the street. On seeing him approaching them, the quarter took the cycle and started rolling it away in haste. Since they did not hear any shouts or calls, they stopped and looked back. What they saw halted them in their tracks. The boy was laughing and waving to them. So they turned back and confronted the boy.

They wanted to know what was so funny about the theft of a bicycle and why he was laughing instead of raising an alarm. The boy could not stop laughing. Catching back his breath, he told them that the cycle belonged to his old school teacher who had received this bicycle in dowry at the time of his marriage.

About a year ago the boy and his friends had taken the cycle and given it to a scrap merchant for free but the man returned it saying it was useless and worthless. So when he saw them stealing it, he was happy that at last the old man will have to give up on the bicycle. Chikku wanted to know whether the old man would report the theft to the police. The boy laughed again and said that if he did, the police would throw him behind the bars for unnecessarily disturbing them.

Much to the boy's disappointment they put the cycle back and walked their way back to their usual meeting place under the tree. They were now convinced that they were in a crisis and that desperate situations demanded desperate actions, but the problem was they didn't know what it was.

JP suddenly said that he had a monstrous idea but was not very comfortable with it. The others were not much enthused but nevertheless wanted to know what the idea was. JP looked around uneasily and having satisfied himself that there was no one within ear shot said that messing with a female would certainly land them in trouble but was not sure whether it would get them to the prison as the matter may not be reported to the police.

Mano disagreed and said that he knew all about women and asked them to leave it to him. So he told Chikku to first go and find a girl. Chikku wanted to know of what age. Mano said 20 would be fine. So off went Chikku in search of a girl of 20 they could mess with.

But he returned almost immediately and said he had a doubt. Mano was getting tired of this fellow and said "What?" Chikku wanted to know if he could not find one of 20, whether 2 of 10 would do. As Mano picked up stones to pelt him, he exited hastily.

It was nearly two hours since he was gone which made the other three wonder if it was so difficult to find a girl of 20 in this town. Kabali remarked that everything seemed to be difficult somehow. Then they saw Chikku walking briskly with a broad smile on his face. He seemed quite excited too.

When he saw that they were eager to know what he had to say, he thought he would play them up a bit. He started telling them how difficult it was to find girls outside in this town and how they always kept indoors and seldom came out and how he had to go from place to place trying to peep inside houses and so on and on. He was clearly beating around the bush. Quite unexpectedly, JP caught him by the throat and almost strangled him.

Mano and Kabali intervened and asked him to come to the point.

Chikku was not a guy who would give up his ways so easily. So he said that they had to have patience and in fact they should congratulate him for not finding just a girl of 20 but for finding perhaps the most beautiful girl in town. Then he went on to describe her in great detail.

Once he was done, Mano said with a solemn expression that it was not good. In fact the choice was quite bad as it could land them in serious trouble. JP, who by now was feeling quite elated about the girl demanded to know what was so bad. Mano said, the girl this idiot just described was Kavita, the daughter of the local police chief DSP Rajasekar.

On hearing this, JP was thrilled and said Chikku had found the best possible girl. He asked them to recall what he had said earlier. Generally people did not go to the police if someone messed with their girl. They either beat you up or locked up the girl but would never go to the police. So the chances of going to the prison for it were bleak. But if the girl happened to be the daughter of a policeman, they would certainly throw you into the can. You may have to take some beating but at least it will get you in and keep you in for a while. After all that is what they had been struggling to do so far.

Mano and Kabali felt quite squeamish about the idea and did not want to be a part of it in anyway. On seeing the fear in their eyes, Chikku too developed cold feet and said he agreed with Mano. JP was quite annoyed at the turn of events. Just when a workable plan was falling in place, these jokers chose to act funny. So, he told them that if that is what they wanted, it was fine with him. He would go it alone. He asked Chikku to just show him the girl and where to find her, he would take care of the rest.

JP was quite a handsome fellow unlike the other three who were quite ordinary in looks, physique and manners. JP was way above them and was an attractive guy with some manners. He could pass off for an educated guy as long as he kept his mouth shut. He was good at sweet talking too and was confident of impressing girls with his macho looks.

Chikku showed him where the girl lived and even pointed her out, which was not required really speaking. Then his part was over. JP was alone from now on and the other three faded away.

To begin with JP started stalking Kavita and it did not go unnoticed. The girl started taking note of him, and that soon resulted in eye contact. But he kept his distance and was discreet. One day she happened to be walking back home alone and the street was deserted but for this handsome guy leaning on the lamp post and smoking. It was the same guy Kavita had been noticing for a while. As she passed him, she stole a sideways glance and in the process tripped on the stone and fell forward. JP who was waiting for an opportunity like this rose to the occasion and caught her in time and prevented the fall that could have hurt her badly.

When he steadied her, she said a meek 'thanks' and ran off not bothering to pick up the footwear that had come off. JP picked up the pair of slippers. The strap of one of them had snapped. He took it to a cobbler and got the slipper mended. The next day he saw her coming and placed the slippers packed neatly in a newspaper in her path and walked away. Kavita, having noticed it, picked it up casually and walked away but not without looking through the corner of her eyes to see if he was looking at her.

Now the eye contact became regular and whenever possible a smile was exchanged too. The exchanges escalated to lip reading words mouthed in silence. Then started their secret rendezvous. It was a huge road side tree with a large trunk that had a deep depression that could hide two people and faced the thick bushes and not the road. It was a very convenient spot that was unnoticeable from the road on either side of the tree.

The plan had gone wrong. He was meeting her secretly and did not wish to get caught for he had fallen in love and so had the girl. Many times he tried to convince himself but in vain that it was not true and that he was only pursuing a plan to go to prison. Soon he realized that he could not fool himself and that he was madly in love with her. So, he decided to tell her everything. He told her the truth that he was a petty thief and that after seeing her had turned over a new leaf and was now looking for a decent job so that one day he could walk up to her father and ask for her hand.

In the mid 1960s there were no unknown secrets in a small town and their secret meetings were no exceptions. Word got around to DSP Rajasekar and his wife. When she wanted to thrash the girl and lock her up, he said no and asked her to leave it to him. He knew how to nip such things in the bud discreetly.

JP's 'friends', the trio too observed him from a safe distance. He was now going about town looking for a job. Taking turns each of them bumped into him at different places and at different times and warned him and asked him to back off before it was too late. But he was beyond repair. He wouldn't listen to anything, least of all reason.

One day, when JP and Kavita were cozily cuddled against each other inside the tree trunk, quite unexpectedly, two constables appeared as if out of nowhere. By instinct, the girl ducked, covered her face and sped from the place. One of the constables asked the other to search JP. They had blocked his way such that there was no escape. Since JP did not have anything to conceal, he let the constable search him. The constable after searching his shirt pockets and finding nothing asked him to raise his hands and started searching his pant pockets. JP had nothing in them anyway. So, didn't mind it.

The constable after searching the last pocket showed the other senior constable what he had found. He was holding a packet of poppy seeds (ganja). Even before JP could begin his protests, the senior constable snapped the hand cuff and started pushing him to the station. When he tried to resist, the two constables together dragged him to the police station.

At the station JP was booked for possession of narcotic drugs. He cried hoarse that it was not true and that he had been framed but in vain. When DSP Rajasekar arrived, JP pleaded that he was innocent and prayed to let him go as he was not guilty. He did not want to go to prison.

The DSP told him with a triumphant grin that there was no point in crying now. He should have thought about it earlier before getting himself into serious trouble. It was too late now.

The trio had seen the whole episode and lamented that had he heeded to their advice, he would not have ended up like this. Mano commented that it was strange how the human mind worked and said" JP was struggling hard to go to prison and chose a path. After succeeding, he doesn't want it."

Chikku got philosophical and said that no one can escape the Hand of Fate.

TO TIE OR NOT TO TIE

"Preetha," called Anil again but there was no response still. So he shook her by the shoulder and called again. "Anil? What is it?" she quipped. "Wonderful," continued Anil, "I should be the one asking you that question. Anyway, if you are finished let's go, it is nearly 7.00 already."

As they packed their bags and left the office, he said, "What were you dreaming about anyway?" It was quite dark and a tad chill for a mid November evening. "I was not dreaming," she said and suggested they stop by for a cup of hot coffee. Anil could never say no to coffee and was game to it anytime, anywhere. So they made it to their usual haunt. The aroma and the first sip warmed her up and she started to say something but then stopped. Anil, who was watching her, urged her to go on and say it. She shook her head and said he wouldn't understand. He felt hurt. They had known each other for seven years through college and later at work. He thought they understood each other very well. The coffee felt suddenly cold and tasteless. She saw the sick dog look on his face and realized her mistake. "Sorry, I didn't mean it that way. Anyway, it is nothing, chodo, chaltey hain," she said cheerfully patting his back, as usual.

They walked back to their home. They had hired two single room flats facing each other and shared it with a roommate each. Preetha's roommate was Anita, a happy go lucky chatter box who believed in enjoying every moment of life. Though it was quite taxing sometimes, Preetha liked her because she was a nice person, very kind and always ready to help. She always teased Anil to his discomfort and Preetha's amusement. Anil's roommate Kishore was a shy guy who seldom spoke on his own to anyone, least of all to girls, whom he avoided. Anil liked him as he was unobtrusive and almost invisible, even though he woke up very early and also went to bed early unlike

Anil who always kept late nights and woke up late. He had a passion for cleanliness and kept the room spotlessly clean, so Anil didn't have to bother about it. The walk back was mostly silent though Preetha tried her bit to cheer him up. They bid goodnight and retired to their rooms.

The next morning turned out to be dull and grey and quite cold. So, Preetha, who normally reached the office at least 15–20 minutes early, was late today. When she rushed out, she bumped into Anil, who as usual was rushing out at the last moment. Anil always took a cab and Preetha joined him. The short journey passed in silence. The weather didn't help either. On reaching the office they just waved to each other and rushed off to their seats. The day turned out to be long and hectic with heavy workload leaving no time for the usual small talk during lunch and tea breaks. Around 6 p.m, Preetha looked up and was surprised to see Anil standing there silently watching her. Without saying a word, he just showed her his watch. She gestured back to say 5 minutes. By the time she wound up it was 6.30. They walked in silence involuntarily to the café and sat at their usual table. Then Anil said, "So, I don't understand." She said, "Oh my God, now I understand why you have been sulking. Come on I told you, it is nothing." He didn't accept that and went on to say that he had been observing her and that of late something had been bothering her which she was not sharing with him. She became serious and asked him, "OK, tell me. Why do people marry?"

The question both surprised and amused Anil, he started laughing and said, "What a stupid question?" Then he went on to ask her, "Why do people go to school or college or work, and why do people eat, drink, make merry, watch films, sing songs, attend parties." He finally concluded that it was just a natural thing. When you grow up, you get married and raise a family. She sat through looking at him and when he was finally finished, she said, "That's why I said you won't understand."

She continued, "Look Anil, you are a nice guy, you were good at studies, you are good at work, you are good with numbers, you are kind and friendly, you like peace, you respect elders and are well behaved, and I like you for what you are. We are good friends and have known each other well all these seven years. To you everything is natural. So when people marry it is natural, if they are unhappy, it is natural. If they separate or divorce, it is natural. You never think why it should be so because you don't have the wisdom. That's why I said you won't understand."

He was totally stunned by the way she said it more than what she had said. She said it so calmly like a mother to a child trying to tell him that he was not grown up enough to understand the ways of the world. Suddenly he felt that he didn't know her at all though he had known her for seven long years. He felt he was sitting with a stranger. He didn't know what to say to her.

Before he could think of something to say, she spoke. She said, "I am sorry Anil. I apologize for what I said but I couldn't help speak the truth. But then I need to explain."

She went on to tell him why she was bothered by that question, "Why do people marry?"

She had gone with Anita to her place the previous week-end to celebrate her sister's divorce. Preetha felt quite uncomfortable with the idea and was not keen to go. But when Anita insisted, she could not refuse. Anita was good looking and smart but she paled compared to her sister Sarita, who was very beautiful, well educated, working as an officer in a private bank, quite composed and carried herself with dignity. Unlike Anita, she never spoke more than necessary and had a patient ear to anyone who spoke. She was also a good singer and an excellent cook. Any match maker would die to find such a 'catch'. She had married a very tall and handsome engineer with an MBA from IIMA, who had risen to the top in a large business concern in double quick time. He was highly respected and regarded for his sharp mind and swift and shrewd decisions. In the eyes of matchmakers he was an equally good 'catch'. Yet the marriage had failed and resulted in a divorce that called for a 'celebration'.

When they got married, they looked every bit a perfect match and an ideal pair so much so that they were envied by people young and old alike. But then there was a major problem no one knew about. In all the 5 years of their married life they did not have any sexual relationship because he was incapable of one. It came as a rude shock to her the very first night of their marriage, but Sarita being what she was never spoke about this to anyone, not even to her parents. Her in-laws soon learnt about it and turned the table on her and branded her impotent. To make matters worse, verbal abuses, physical torture and ill-treatment followed. It soon grew out of proportions as they were emboldened by her silent suffering. But on the surface, everything looked hunky dory. It soon started affecting her professional life. It was then that she took one bold and firm step. She called her husband and told him she was not returning home and that her lawyer would send him the divorce notice. She went to her parents' home and told them everything and that she had come back to stay. They were shocked beyond words but understood because they always adored her for her level headedness and pragmatic decisions.

Her in-laws too realized the futility of a fight and also feared the publicity that may follow. So they gave in for a divorce by mutual consent. The lawyers met, chalked out a workable petition and moved the court for a favourable decision. It went through without a noise.

So Sarita's family decided to celebrate her liberation from the tortures of an unhappy marriage and in appreciation of the way she had handled the whole thing on her own. Preetha felt happy that she had joined in. You seldom get a chance to meet people like Sarita. Preetha wondered why Sarita had endured the torture for so long and had not taken the bold step earlier.

The next day (Sunday) when Preetha found herself alone in the company of Sarita, she brought it up. Sarita explained why. At first she felt very miserable but later realized that he must be feeling even more so. She felt very sorry for him and so reconciled herself to the situation. She then had a heart to heart chat with him and told him she would never utter a word about it. He appreciated her and even adored her for her understanding and care. So they lived quite happily for some time, i.e., until the family realized that there was going to be no children from this marriage. So to hide the truth and to respond to the wagging tongues, they put the blame on her. She still didn't mind. She tried hard to make the marriage work but then there was a limit to everything.

She then went on to tell her about her specialist lawyer and narrated the numerous divorce cases handled by her. She then told her how people have started applying for divorce at the drop of a hat and of the countless hasty marriages and hastier divorces. She narrated several cases. Preetha was dumbfounded. It baffled her as to why people marry in the first place.

"Now tell me, Anil. Why do people marry?" asked Preetha. This time he did not laugh. He didn't have an answer this time. It no longer seemed a 'natural thing' to him. They sat in silence, their coffees cold and untouched. Their thoughts were interrupted by an "excuse me" from a gentleman now standing by their table. He pulled up a chair and sat down as he said "May I?" They were too confused to say anything. So, he continued, "My sincere apologies for barging in on your conversation. After hearing everything, I could not keep myself from imposing upon you. I did not overhear. You weren't whispering anyway."

Preetha was quick to recover and said, "So you want to tell us why people marry, Mr……?"

"Triloknath Das," completed the gentleman. He went on to narrate thus but not without saying, "With your kind permission."

"It is nearly four decades since we tied the knot. It would be a blatant lie to say that it feels like yesterday because it isn't true.

It has been a long and pleasant journey with the inevitable quota of pains and losses. We are grateful to all our well wishers and equally, if not more, to those who are not so inclined. Thanks to mortal men and immortal Gods and their blessings, we have had a happy life and hope for the same in the remaining years.

We are the blessed ones and that makes scores of others jealous of us. Neither they nor we can help it. We feel sorry for them. We pray to God to make their lives happier. Not because they will stop being jealous of us but because everyone is entitled to happiness.

We have wondered why some people are unhappy about others being happy. It is perhaps because they see others' lives from outside and their own from inside. They look at what the others have and what they themselves have not and thus live in a frequent state of unhappiness.

If we are content with what we have, there is no scope for unhappiness."

"How's that possible, Uncle?" chipped in Preetha.

"It is simpler said than done, agreed. No two individuals (or couple) are alike and so are their lives. When we expect them to be alike, at par (or better), problems arise. When simple expectations turn into needs, wants, desires, ambitions, aspirations and obsessions, life becomes complex.

Being social animals, we cannot escape the interplay of complexities of individuals whether or not they are in any way related to us. How well we cope with it determines the quality of our lives.

Every individual has a right to lead a life as he or she pleases. Others have the right to only guide or advise (only if called for) an individual, unless he or she is living off them. As long as we are children or young adults dependent on our parents or guardians, we cannot deny them their right to monitor or determine what we could or could not do because they are responsible for our lives.

Once we turn into self supporting adults, we certainly have the right to make our life choices. In reality, most of us are not adequately prepared to handle our own lives when we reach this stage. Merely drawing hefty sums of money or attaining physical maturity does not make us competent to make life choices unless we have a level head on our shoulders."

"Why does everyone target the present generation?" said Preetha a little acidly.

"No..." he dragged. "Preetha," she completed.

"No, Preetha, you are mistaken. I am not targeting any generation in particular," he said and continued. "Don't forget, every generation has drawn heftier salaries than the previous one. My father had never dreamt of the kind of salaries I have drawn and you will draw more than I have ever."

"Now, where was I?" Das said, a bit lost.

"We were on the subject of marriage, Uncle," reminded Preetha.

"Yes, Marriage," he continued, "Marriage is an important turning point in one's life. It is the beginning of one's own family life. So one needs to be prepared to face a host of problems and responsibilities and take care of them (precisely what the parents or guardians did earlier). It is the beginning of two people deciding to live together in order to fulfill their desires and dreams. So the need to understand your life partner's needs, ideas, likes, dislikes, tastes and so on and so forth and align yours to them becomes paramount.

When we enter into an alliance, we vow to care and share our joys and sorrows with our life partner. It makes no difference whether the life partner was chosen by us (love marriage) or by our parents (arranged marriage). There is no guarantee as to which one succeeds and which fails."

"So, what makes a marriage tick or trip?" asked Anil finding his voice at last and joining the conversation.

"VOW, it is the vow," said Das with a gleam in his eyes and looked askance at him.

"He is Anil," said Preetha by way of introduction.

"Thank you Preetha," said Das and continued addressing Anil, "The most important point is how serious are we about it. That determines the fate of our marriage. It is purely a question of commitment. But invariably people ask, "Why should I compromise?" as if it is a border dispute between India and Pakistan.

"So, why do people marry?" said Preetha reminding him of her question.

"Yes, yes, I am coming to it," said Das and continued, "People marry for a variety of reasons and most people get married for all the wrong reasons. Parents' compulsion, to pave way for younger siblings, what will society say; love at first sight, liking each other, premarital pregnancy and so on and on.

There are also a number of people who marry to have children and raise a family or just to prove their potency to the society and then like our friend said, 'it is a natural thing to do'," said Das with a faint smile on his lips. Anil was not amused, especially since Preetha chuckled.

"I tell you," declared Das, "There is nothing natural about marriage. It is as unnatural as all the other natural things we do – digging up the earth for minerals and oils, destroying forests for cultivation, then converting agricultural land to housing complexes to live in artificial dwellings, raising live stock only to slaughter them and the list can go on, but the most unnatural thing is cooking our food and wearing clothes."

"Come on, Uncle," said Anil, "How can we go around naked, eating raw meat like savages? We are civilized people."

"That," said Das, "is the problem, dear. Don't forget, that is precisely how our ancestors lived and they were a happy lot and for your information there are some tribes who live even today like that happily and our governments are hell bent on 'civilizing' them.

What is natural is a sexual intercourse between a male and a female of every species on earth. No species, except man, indulges in indiscriminate and frequent intercourse. Only man has made it a pervert act and indulges in rape and has made sex a trade and the female a commodity. Only man indulges in orgies and other perversions like masturbation.

So, in order to protect our children from being drawn into such perversions and pave the way for fulfilling a legitimate biological need, our ancestors who formed societies invented 'marriage' as a ritual to sanctify a relationship between a man and a woman so that they can live together caring for each other and sharing their joys and sorrows and satisfying their sexual needs without shame. In fact it is encouraged. So parents start eagerly looking forward to the birth of a child and keep asking the young couple when they can hear the good news.

Like I said before, we live in a complex world and it is possible that at times the husband or the wife or both may be drawn to someone else of the opposite sex. I mean find someone else attractive. It is quite natural. If we give in, we destroy the sanctity of marriage and break the VOW we took at the time of marriage.

Marriage is not just the tying of the knot. It is the tying of two lives together. It is a sacred institution of discipline, self restraint and a commitment to caring and sharing. So it is very important to take utmost care in choosing your life partner to ensure the success of your marriage."

"How can we be sure whether our choice is right, especially when marriages are arranged by parents and the partner is a total stranger," questioned Preetha.

Das laughed and said, "That reminds me of an article I read last week in one of the leading dailies. The girl wrote in the column that marriage should be solemnized only after ensuring 100% compatibility between the boy and the girl. Even the numerous gadgets you people use so extensively are not guaranteed for 100% compatibility, be it the hardware or the software. How can two people with complexities of likes and dislikes be 100% compatible?

Success of a marriage depends on the lifelong commitment of the partners to each other and to their marriage. Couples who do so are generally hailed as made for each other."

"So, I hope I have answered your question," said Das and continued, "Oh my, it is nearly 9.00. Let's order something to eat. The treat is on me. I have to thank you for patiently hearing me."

All three felt quite hungry after all the heavy talk, and after refreshing themselves attacked the hot rotis and side dishes they had ordered.

Das continued his sermon before parting and said, "One more thing about unnatural things being legitimized as natural. It is the gay marriage. It is termed as marriage because of their commitment to each other even though their sexual relation is not natural. There is nothing wrong about that. For that matter it is equally right for a person to choose to be single, a spinster/bachelor for life. It only means that you are not committing yourself to another person. So are live in relationships. What is so wrong about them, nothing. Think about it," saying so he bid them good night and left.

On the way back to their rooms, Preetha said, "Anil, what do you think?" Pat came his reply, "Lots of gas. What about you?"

She took her time and as they reached their doors, she said, "I am confused. I am in a dilemma."

Dismayed, Anil asked, "What is it now?" She said, "To Tie, or Not To Tie."

Without a word Anil vanished behind the door leaving Preetha with her dilemma.